The Banyan Tree

VINAY CHAKRAVARTHY

ISBN 978-93-5559-033-6

First published in India 2022 by Leadstart Inkstate
A brand of One Point Six Technologies Pvt. Ltd.

123, Building J2, Shram Seva Premises,
Wadala Truck Terminal,
Mumbai 400022, Maharashtra, INDIA
Phone: +91 96999 33000
Email: info@leadstartcorp.com
www.leadstartcorp.com

Disclaimer: This is a work of fiction. All the names, characters, businesses, places, events and incidents in this book are either the product of the author's imagination or used in a fictitious manner. Any resemblance to actual persons, living or dead, or actual events is purely coincidental

Editor: Vaibhav Pathare
Cover: Swapnil Behere
Layouts: Kevis Tech

This book is dedicated to my wife, Harini, and children Aditi and Dhruv, who have encouraged me to keep writing and been my sounding board. My parents have struggled through much to give me opportunities and my siblings have always been there for me. I am eternally grateful to them.

"The distinction between the past, present and future is only a stubbornly persistent illusion."

Albert Einstein

Contents

Chapter 1

This is a story that begins in India. Not of modern malls and megaplex cinemas, not even of the British. Not the Mughals and Marathas, but even further back. Imagine a country dotted with thousands of kingdoms amidst lush forests, where the lines between real and unreal, magic and reality were far blurrier than they are today. A world where everything was not always as it seemed. Traveling between kingdoms could be treacherous, taking the traveler down lonely paths and dark forests with no hotels, no cars, and far from the nearest Kingdom. Where magic and other worlds felt emboldened to show themselves.

On one such journey was Kautilya. He had not wanted to be on this trip, but there was no other way. His father had insisted and he had been too proud to tell him otherwise. Too proud to tell him he was scared to travel alone on this lonely road. Too proud to tell him of the stories he had heard of famous dacoits and clever ghosts.

His family members were successful gemstone traders in Pochampally, and his father had made a transaction with a trader in the neighboring kingdom of Koshala. Kautilya had been chosen against his wishes to complete the transaction, exchanging their rubies for diamonds.

The road was getting more deserted. It was still paved, but the cobblestones were getting less orderly as Kautilya left the kingdom. Soon it would disappear altogether, the road becoming nothing more than a large, wide path in the woods. The woods in this part of India were mostly low brush interspersed with peepal, jamun, and banyan trees.

The King's guard patrolled the area and made sure it was accessible for the first 20 miles or so outside the main gates. But after that, it was mostly maintained by the tread of feet, by man and beast. Every 20 to 30 miles or so one could sometimes find a serai, a wayside inn of sorts that would provide a simple hot meal and provisions, but he knew the path he was on didn't have one for at least the first 90 miles. He had planned accordingly; his mother had packed him some rice, dal, and vegetables for the way, and that would keep him for at least a few days. He had enough water for a day, but he hoped he would come across a stream by the second day. The monsoon had been drier than usual and he wondered if the streams would have dried up by now. Maybe he would run into another wayfarer coming the other way with more water. Thinking about the water was already making him thirsty. *I must go slow with it*, he thought.

Soon he was past all his usual landmarks, crossing the old stone bridge and the ruins of the ancient temple. The temple had always given him the creeps, and Kautilya recalled always reciting the Hanuman Chalisa as he passed by it as a boy. Soon he would see the round arch, a memorial of some old victory, now forgotten, and that would be as far as he had ever been in his life. His father had told him to go to the path on the right of that archway, and from then on it was more or less straight going till he reached Koshala. It was straight going, yes, but walking 90 miles through the jungle was something that he wasn't looking forward to. But he knew it was time to prove himself. By 15 his brother had already been to Kalinga at least once and perhaps even to Koshala.

He had probably come about 10 miles out of the city and was tired, so he sat down. The sun was in the western part of the sky; Kautilya guessed it was probably late afternoon. He could probably go another five or seven miles before sunset, he thought, taking a sip of water. The jungle was slowly encroaching up on the road now, the wild bramble becoming thicker as he went. This was soon going to be tiger country, and he was hoping to run into a fellow traveler so he could have both company and safety. A traveler that spoke Prakrit would be even better. As the evening wore on, the darkness began to close in as the sun reached lower on the horizon. Soon, he approached a large Banyan tree, its branches radiating at least 100 meters around it. It had probably been here for hundreds of years or more, he thought. This would be a good place to spend the night. There was just enough light to gather twigs and make a fire. He had some rice and vegetables in his bag and was looking forward to a nice warm meal. As he started gathering twigs and branches, he heard a noise behind him!

Now, if you've never seen a banyan tree, they are a magnificent sight, with the roots that hang and the branches that spread wide. If you have seen one, you will also know that they are a creepy sight at night. The noise in the branches was real. Kautilya nearly jumped, but calmed himself, reciting the Hanuman Chalisa as he turned around. He saw an old woman coming from behind the Banyan tree. She must've just been sitting on the other side of the tree, he thought. She looked like she was more than 100 years old. Her skin was shriveled, and she hunched over, a crooked stick for support. She appeared to be blind but moved surely in his direction.

"Is someone there?" she said in Prakrit.

"Yes," replied Kautilya, "I am here."

"Oh, thank God," she said. "It is you," she said in a familiar manner.

"Do you know me?" he asked.

"Tell him…Not now…He isn't ready…If not now when?… Now! Now! Now! No!" She yelled.

Kautilya stepped back, shocked. "I'm sorry, are you talking to me?"

"He... he," she cackled "Yes, yes I am... now."

Kautilya looked closer at the woman, in the fading light, her skin was dark like wrinkled paper. Darker brown splotches covered her face, she had a kind smile, more like a toothless grin. Her eyes seemed to flicker.

"What are you doing here?" said Kautilya, once he got over his initial shock of seeing her and realized she was harmless… just an old woman. Probably lost, he thought, but how did she get here?

As if reading his mind, she said, "I was lost on the way to Kalinga and have been hoping someone would come by to help."

"How did you get here by yourself?" asked Kautilya. "I came here with my son," she said, gesturing with her stick.

Only then did Kautilya notice a rather measly-looking dog lying amongst the roots of the Banyan tree. It was a sickly looking mongrel.

"But I thought you said your son," he said. "I only see your dog laying there. Nobody else is around."

"Son…Yes…dog, right, dog," she said. "That's right, my dog," she cackled again.

Kautilya was now getting hungry and moved to take his food out of the bag. He probably would have to share it with the old woman, he thought, not entirely pleased. Again, as if reading his mind, she said, "I can help you make a fire." "Oh, don't worry about it," said Kautilya. "I was just gathering some branches when I saw you. You can just sit here," he said.

Kautilya bent down and began to gather branches and twigs and put them in a large pile a few feet away from the Banyan tree. "Do you have any food?" she asked. Kautilya thought again about the few pounds of rice he had, and the distance he had to travel, but still said yes. "I was just going to boil some rice and vegetables," he said. "That sounds delicious," she said and sat down on her haunches as her dog limped up to her. How did she get here? he thought as he gathered up twigs, blind as she was, and with just the mangy dog for company.

Maybe she was abandoned by her family, he thought. As he turned to walk back down to the banyan tree, he saw the flickering light of a fire. He had to search a little for dry twigs. There had been a light rain the day before and some of the wood was still damp, by the time he returned the old woman was hunched over a fire muttering to herself. She seemed to be saying words in a language he couldn't understand. How did she get the fire going? thought Kautilya.

"How did you get the fire going?" he asked bewildered, as there wasn't enough wood and also no provision to light it with? "Oh, just this and that," she said. Still puzzled, Kautilya kept his eyes on her as he took out a little pot and set it on the fire with the help of stones. He put some water and rice and vegetables on it to boil. "Son… What's your name?" she asked. "Kautilya," he said. "Kautilya, what a nice name. I knew a Kautilya once…" she trailed off. "Kautilya, I have troubled you a lot but can I ask you another favor, I have my things in a bag. Can you get it for me? I am old and weak and would appreciate it." "I will be glad to help," he said. "Where is your bag?" he asked. "It's on the tree on the third branch." "On the tree! How did you get it up on the tree!" he asked shocked. "My son helped me," she said. "I didn't want any bandits to get my things." "Your son?" "Yes," she said, again pointing to the dog. Kautilya now began to think that she was a little senile or crazy or both! "Are you sure it's on the tree?" "Yes," she said, sounding exasperated. "Of course, it is!" "I put it there and I have all my things and I need my medicine that the Vaidya gave me for my joint aches and they hurt so much!" Can you please help an old woman and get me the medicine?"

"Can't we finish eating first?" said Kautilya.

The old woman sighed deeply and said, "Well, if you can't get it now that's fine."

He could see that she wouldn't stop and he finally relented and looked up the tree. It didn't look too difficult to climb and with all the hanging roots he would be able to get up there easily. I might as well humor her, otherwise, she won't let me eat in peace, he thought. "But are you sure it's on the third branch?" "Yes, of course, it is," she said.

He tried to put out of his mind all the stories he had heard about haunted banyan trees. It was said that mischievous spirits hung around Banyan trees, waiting to attach themselves to unsuspecting travelers. It was just an old wives' tale, told to keep children from wandering off at night he thought. The tale of Vikram and Betal came to his mind. He was certainly no Vikram and hoped there was no Betal on this tree. He climbed up the tree; it was not unlike the many he had climbed growing up near his house. The light from the fire flickered in the branches and roots, casting an eerie light and the shadows danced especially as the light hit the multiple roots that hung from the tree. He could hear the woman muttering to herself and laughing intermittently, she's not all there he thought.

"Third branch right!" he shouted down towards the woman. "Yes!" she said. It wasn't a difficult climb at all, but it would've been a lot easier if the light was better and if he could slow his heart down, which was beating out of his chest. Ghoulish visions from childhood nightmares danced in his head. Second branch, just one more to go… "Ow!" he said as he scraped his knee on a broken branch. It felt like a superficial scrape but he could feel some blood running down his right leg. The sooner this thing was done with the better, he thought as he pulled himself up onto the third branch. He was now a good 25 feet or more off the ground. He saw a white shadow at the end of the branch, probably the old woman's bundle. He slid slowly to the edge and reached for the bundle… It seemed to be right in front of him but when he reached for it wouldn't come into his hand. He crept further and reached as far as he could stretch… Suddenly he was falling… Darkness all around, falling for what seemed to be an eternity through the darkness. The darkness was broken only by the woman's cackling, "He! He!" He would surely break his neck or at least a few bones, falling from this high up. He braced for an impact that never seemed to come. He finally hit the bottom and bounced right up, again he fell, again he bounced right up, down again for what seemed an eternity. What was this? The floor was not hard at all but supple! It was in a brightly lit room lit not with torches, but with weird intense light tubes. He saw other boys and girls jumping all around him laughing loudly. "Hey, Amit! do a flip," one of them shouted looking right at him.

"Amit, I'm talking to you man! What's up with you? Did you hit your head?"

He surprised himself as he answered in an unknown language, "No, you idiot, watch me!" he said and he flipped.

Chapter 2

What was this language? Kautilya felt like he was floating outside his own body as though bewitched. He spoke a bizarre language. Was he possessed? Had there been a playful ghost named Amit in the banyan tree that had entered him? He continued to chatter in this unknown language with the boys around him. They were dressed in strange clothes. Blue pajamas that were thick and heavy with some, perhaps the poorer amongst them, with tears in them. Slowly this out-of-body feeling dissipated. The thoughts of Kautilya faded. Amit continued to jump with his friends on the trampoline in the indoor trampoline park, doing tricks with his friends. He moved to the next room to play basketball on the trampoline, managing to get several baskets in. Soon the only feeling he had was a bit of a headache. Had he been jumping too long? Amit turned to his friend Rohit as he put on his shoes.

"Hey, let's go get some ice cream!" It was Rohit's birthday and his parents had let Rohit, Amit and a few of their other friends have an evening out at the indoor trampoline park, a favorite of theirs for the last year or so, since it opened. Rohit said, "Let's get some pizza first." "Sure," said Amit. They sat eating some oily not-so-great pizza at the food court. It was a cold Saturday in November in Valparaiso. The sun would soon start to go down, though it was only 3:30 PM or so. Soon the time change would start and winter would too. Last winter had been quite bad or good, I guess depending on your perspective. His parents had complained about the difficult drive in the snow. His friends on the other hand had loved having three snow days as well, as plenty of time, snowboarding in the neighborhood park.

He was 18 and college applications would start soon. It had been a long hard year, with plenty of classwork to do. In a few months, he would have to decide as to which college he would go to, as well as choose a major. The stress of decision making was getting to him and he had not been sleeping very well as a result. The sleepless nights thinking about what he would do were wearing him down.

Amit and his friends finished their ice cream. They picked up their things from the locker and he texted his mother to come and pick them up as his friends did the same. He pulled his hood on to protect himself against the chilly November air. It was already 30°F and would only get colder from here on.

His mother pulled up in the minivan and he got in. She looked at him quizzically, "Are you all right?" she asked. "Yes, I think I was jumping too much. I have a headache," Amit said. "Let's go home and I can make you some tea," said his mother. They drove silently to their house in the next suburb. They had moved here eight years ago from Dallas and he had hated it at first, especially missing leaving his friends in Dallas with whom he had grown up. He was born in Dallas but when his mother was laid off, they were forced to move. Amit hated the cold and leaving all his friends but had grown to love his new school, and made friends with Rohit and Isaiah. They were brought together initially, by the love of the World of Warcraft and were now inseparable. He remembered his first few days at middle school, he was a shy boy but fortunately found himself sitting next to Rohit on the bus. He happened to be reading Percy Jackson and the Lightning Thief and Amit couldn't help but start a conversation about the book which he loved passionately. This led them to bond over their love of all things of Greek mythology. Isaiah had been Rohit's friend from Elementary school and the three soon became fast friends. Rohit and Isaiah had both decided that they wanted to go into pre-med. His parents hoped he would choose medicine too, but he had resisted. He was still unsure as to which direction he wanted to go. Both his parents were from a scientific background, his father had done Material sciences and taught at the local university and his mother was an engineer at the local steel plant. As they drove into their neighborhood, he smiled at the wistful names that hoped to evoke a sense of the woods. Something that he and his father found amusing was the cedarwood and briarwood lanes. Funniest of all, Garland Circle! *Wasn't that somewhat redundant?* His father would often ask. Both a Garland and a Circle.

As he walked in the front door, he saw his father watching TV, a cricket match was on. "Hi! Amit, how was your party?" he said.

"It was good," said Amit, his father turned and looked at him.

"You don't look well, are you OK?" "That's what I said" his mother agreed.

"I was jumping too much, I think I have a headache," he explained again.

"Do you want to sit down and watch the match with me?" His dad asked him eagerly. He had been trying to get him and his sister interested in cricket for as long as Amit could remember.

Amit laughed, "No thanks! That might make the headache worse. I'm just going to go to my room and read and go to bed." Amit took off his jacket and shoes and went up to his bedroom. His room still had the old Minecraft posters on the wall. *You really should take those down,* his friends teased incessantly. They were all obsessed with Minecraft at one time but had moved on. He was the only one who had not taken down the posters. They were comforting to him in some way. The bed was warm and inviting, and he pulled up the covers not bothering to change. He felt strangely exhausted, drained. He tried to read for a little but felt his eyes closing and drifted off to sleep. Downstairs, Manoj, Amit's father, turned off the TV. "I'm worried about him," he said to his wife. By this time, Asha had already made up her mind about political science and was working towards getting a college list going. "He just seems so worried and stressed all the time but doesn't seem to make a decision. I just hope he's not depressed," said Kavita. "I've heard that this is a peak period for teenage depression and suicide."

"Yes, that is true. Maybe we should have him see a psychologist," said Manoj.

"How about we have him start meditation again?" said Kavita. "Remember when he was younger, he seemed to enjoy it?"

"What about all the dreams he would complain about? Don't you remember that's why we stopped? He would sleep-talk and mumble and make weird sounds all night," said Manoj.

"That was when he was ten, Maybe it was just a phase, night terrors, perhaps," said Kavita. "The meditation will probably help him focus."

"I hope so. I just remember how freaked out you were about the strange sounds he would make!" said Manoj.

"Ha! Ha! Yes!" said Kavita. "Probably those stupid TV shows he was watching at the time."

"You know what, I think I'm going to do this. get him into meditation classes again at the temple," said Kavita with resolve. "Help him focus a little bit if nothing else..."

The next morning as Amit ate his breakfast, he noticed his father looking at his mother. "Amit," she said, "your dad and I think it would be useful for you to join meditation classes at the temple. They have classes on Friday evenings from 7:30 to 8:30. I don't think you'll need the beginner's class and probably could do the advanced one..."

"Come on mom, I already have so much school stuff to do, I don't want to add one more thing," said Amit.

"Amit, I think this will be calming," said his dad. He could see that this was something that they had discussed and there would not be any wiggle room between them.

"OK, fine. Sign me up. Looks like I don't have a say in this anyway," he said and stomped off to get his backpack.

He had just started driving his father's old Honda to school and he picked up the keys and his backpack as he headed out the door sulkily.

"Bye!" he said, as he slammed the door behind him.

"That went well," said Manoj, as he smiled at Kavita. "Ok, have to run too," he said, as he headed out of the door.

Amit remembered going to meditation classes when he was around 10 or so, he also remembered the immense sense of calm he would feel after, he also recalled the vivid dreams. He wouldn't describe them as nightmares, rather they were so real he could literally feel them. Even before the meditation classes, he had always been able to remember his dreams. Their vividity surprised him especially when friends could barely remember theirs. He would live entire lives in his dreams. Sometimes he was in ordinary lives, in others the lives he lived were far from it. While he didn't reveal it to many friends, not always was he human in these dreams. Some nights he would wake up panting, convinced he was a street dog in a fight to the death, snarling mutts and bared fangs surrounding him. He would wake up startled. Then, there was that one time. He shuddered and put the thought out of his head.

The week wasn't unlike the many high schoolers, assignments, projects, tests and repeat. Sometimes, these weeks ran into each other. He found his mind wandering as he sat in Mr Phelps's class. This was a challenging class and its dry course material, differential calculus, was torturous at the best of times. Unbidden thoughts of another boy, one dressed simply in a coarse white dhoti and kurta came into his mind. He knew somehow that this was Kautilya but had no idea who that was or where he had seen or heard of him. Was he a movie or book character from the many Amar Chitra Katha stories he had read growing up? Why was he in his consciousness now, in calculus class? The hurly-burly of the school week and the constant noise of the school dispelled all thoughts of Kautilya from his brain for the rest of the week. Occasionally as he was about to doze off to sleep at night, he would have a flash of a bizarre memory: a bag of precious gemstones or an ancient fort. The week passed in a roller coaster blur and spat him into Friday. As he drove home from school, he suddenly remembered the meditation class he had been signed up for. Irritation with his parents bubbled inside him. Didn't they realize how busy his life was already?

Fortunately, he didn't have a lot of assignments that week.

As he drove to the meditation classes that Friday, it was like the week had screeched to a halt. His mother had offered to drop him but now that he could drive, he did not take her up on the offer. Alone with his thoughts on the short drive there he regretted not having put up more of a fight with his parents. The town was small but the temple where the meditation classes were held was in the next town about 12 miles away. The traffic, in spite of it being Friday evening, was not bad and it didn't take long to get there. Thank god for small towns. *That drive would have taken an hour in Dallas*, he thought. He pulled onto the temple grounds; the meditation classes were held in the back. He parked, and as he walked, he tried to remember the basics of his previous meditation classes.

Maybe his mother should've signed him into the basic lessons again he thought. As he walked into the classroom, he saw a few other kids his age, some of whom he knew from the temple over the years. Several were the children of his parents' friends and he knew them from parties over the years. None of them were close friends of his though. He smiled at several of them. He also knew Mr Kailash, the teacher. He was a Neuroscientist who had quit his job many years ago. Rumor had it that he had gone to an ashram in Kerala or the Himalayas to study meditation for 5 years and then returned. He had heard his parents talk of him when he had left. He always seemed to emanate a certain calm whenever Amit had seen him, appearing almost serene. Now he mostly taught yoga at the temple, but also did some research at the University Medical School, researching the effects of yoga on the body. The class was about to start and he put away his things and sat down.

Mr Kailash said, "Hi guys! I am glad all of you are here to take this class. It makes me really happy that you have chosen to connect with yourselves as individual souls. Perhaps this may be the most important class you take all week. In fact, I feel this may be the most important class I teach all week. Working with young minds is my greatest blessing."

Mr Kailash allowed them to settle down on their mats and waited calmly for the chattering to die down. "Yoga and meditation are ways for you to take some time to learn to control your senses," he explained.

"The mind is like a chariot and drawn in different directions by the senses. Through meditation, we hope to give you some sense of control and order to the chaos of your mind and its thoughts. As we set our physical bodies into order the mind will follow. I want all of you to relax. Let's start with your toes, your legs, and then your abdomen. Relax your breathing, your face, and finally your mind."

Mr Kailash's calm, reassuring voice helped Amit slowly relax. "Don't struggle to have your mind devoid of thoughts when a thought comes in, watch it go by like a leaf on a stream unexamined." As he began to breathe deeper, Amit could feel his thoughts slowing down. Mr Kailash had said that he would be doing mostly simple stuff in the first class and then would move onto more complex meditation techniques.

He could feel the air slowly going in and out of each nostril, he felt like he was tired. In and out he continued breathing the sensation of falling that he felt startled him, afraid he opened his eyes with a start and looked around everyone around him at their eyes closed including Mr Kailash. He closed his eyes again and began to try to regulate his breathing again. He was afraid of the feeling of falling again and held himself back and as a result, he was not fully relaxed. The class soon ended with Mr Kailash counting backward "four, three, two, one!" Soon everyone opened their eyes, Mr Kailash's eyes lingered for a few seconds longer on Amit.

As they filed out of class with their things, Mr Kailash stopped him. "Amit, how are you feeling?"

"I'm all right," said Amit "I am just a little tired from school and stuff."

"I know about school, but you don't look yourself," he said with a gentle smile.

"No, I'm fine," said Amit.

"See you next week Mr Kailash," said Amit and he walked out of the room. *That was strange, thought Amit. Why would he think something was wrong with him?* He brushed it off and went home.

That night he went out for a movie with his friends. He felt tired and Rohit asked him if he felt well. Amit brushed it off. The movie ended late and by the time Amit got home, it was late but just under the 11 PM curfew, his parents had set. His parents had gone to their rooms. They still seemed to be awake. He could hear the low hum of the TV from their room. He went into his room and changed for bed. As he lay in bed, he grabbed a book, planning on reading a few pages before bed. He slowly drifted off to sleep, the book gently resting on his chest. Suddenly he sat up with a start, just as he was yelling loudly. He didn't recall what he had been saying, the book he had been reading lay on the floor. He could hear footsteps in the hallway and sat up as his dad opened the door.

"Are you OK Amit?" he said. He had a worried look on his face.

"I think I was just dreaming, sorry if I woke you up," he said, still in a daze.

"Do you remember what you said? can you repeat it?" asked his father, a strange look on his face.

"No... I don't remember" said Amit. "Why?" he asked his dad.

"No, it's nothing, go back to sleep," he said, backing out of the room.

The next morning, Amit woke up with a vague headache, as he got dressed and went down to the kitchen to get some coffee, he glanced at his dad in the kitchen, the events of the previous night slowly came to him. His father turned to look at him, he had an odd expression on his face. Amit remembered the expression from the night before. "Why are you looking at me like that dad? What did I say last night?"

"Nothing," said Manoj, "it was just that you were yelling in a language I couldn't understand," said Manoj. "Maybe it was just gibberish!" said Amit.

"It was just that it sounded like an Indian language except, none that I have ever heard, and you don't know any!" said his father. Amit was stunned. He barely spoke Telugu, the language his mother and father spoke, and this had been a source of great disappointment to his parents. He didn't know of any way he would have read or learned any of the other Indian languages, especially one that his father hadn't even heard of.

The week started and went by fast; he soon was into his busy life. Each day blending into a series of class assignments and due dates. The last year of school was hectic as promised, the looming decision he had to make regarding college ate into any free time he had. He spent time researching colleges online any chance he got. He was now seriously considering becoming a psychologist, a decision he had not yet shared with his parents. He wanted to be able to make the decision himself without pressure or influence from outside. The University of Chicago had a great program but it was expensive and he wanted to make sure he qualified for a scholarship before he discussed it with his parents.

Friday came by and as he finished up at school, he walked to his car exhausted. He had been up late trying to make sure he had his medieval history assignment completed in time. He looked forward to unwinding at home watching TV mindlessly, as he was driving home, he remembered, dang it! He had his meditation class today. Why had he let his mother guilt him into signing up? He rushed home, got a light dinner, and headed for class. He resisted his parent's attempts to talk to him, hoping his disapproval would be conveyed by his standoffishness.

As he walked in, he noticed Mr Kailash hadn't arrived yet, there just a few of the other kids were chatting, yoga mats in hand. He caught a few snatches of conversation, "LeBron was awesome last night, did you see that three-pointer?" The conversation died down as Mr Kailash walked in. The other kids and Amit rolled out the yoga mat and sat down.

Mr Kailash said, "Let's move on to something more complex, shall we?" he smiled a gentle smile at Amit. "Today we can start Pranayama. Pranayama consisted of alternating breathing and breath control, this induced better control of the mind and a deeper level of meditation. Amit had never worked with this technique before. As Mr Kailash explained he followed along, soon Mr Kailash's voice drifted away into the distance as he slowly sank into a deeper state of meditation. He felt his body go limp. After what felt like an eternity, he could slowly feel himself getting colder and colder, and soon he was shivering... Wet! He woke up with a start and looked around. It was dark and raining. His coat was wet, his foot hurt and he looked down dumbfounded to see his paw bleeding. He lay cowering in a corner whimpering and yelping in pain.

Chapter 3

The rain was coming down hard now. The dog was in a corner sheltering from the rain under a cardboard box. It had a desperate look in its eyes. It was hurt. Its leg had a gash which was bleeding. It licked at its wound and whimpered softly, occasionally yelping in pain. The rain had been incessant for the last day or so. The dog had last found a half-eaten sandwich the day before and was very hungry. It already had a scrawny look about it, and the wound on the leg didn't help.

The dog looked around the desolate street. It didn't know that this was Hyderabad, the year was 1984. The street that the dog was sheltering in had a beggar lying in the corner. As the dog whimpered, the beggar looked up, as though woken from his sleep. He too was seeking shelter from the rain; he had a plastic tarp over his head. The rain bounced off the tarp with a pattering and splashed all around him. He sat on a jute bag and by his side sat a plastic can for the change that passers-by would throw in. The dog looked at the man. The beggar had kind eyes and seemed to know the dog. He tried to beckon it, but it knew better. If there's one thing a street dog has, it's a good understanding of the cruelty of man. They would often throw stones at it, or drive it away with sticks. The man did seem to have a caring look in his eyes. The dog wavered. Maybe he would have some food. It licked his wounds and thought better of it. The surrounding buildings had faded paint and peeling posters, that fluttered in the falling rain. The posters from movies long forgotten hung limply. Angry faces drawn in multi colors glared from the posters with dramatic titles emblazoned across them.

The thunder had finally died down. The dog was scared of the thunder and was glad that it had finally stopped. It turned around at the sound of footsteps behind. The beggar had gotten up and was walking towards it, whistling and calling. It turned and ran as fast as its limping leg would allow.

It knew there was a dumpster outside a place where people went in and out all evening, the dumpster was full of leftovers. Sometimes good ones, like pieces of chicken and bread. It knew what had held it back so far. It tried to muster up the courage. It had to eat something. Its empty stomach gave it more courage than anything else and it limped its way sticking close to the walls, hoping not to be seen. It knew what it was afraid of, the large vicious brown dog with a half ear ripped off, no doubt in some epic battle with another gang. Half-Ear controlled the alley along with five other strays and was aggressive in guarding its turf. The dumpster was famous in the neighborhood for the food that was found there—not just the quantity but also the quality, large ribs and whole chicken breasts that were barely bitten made their way into the dumpster. The fragrance of the spices wafted for a hundred feet from the dumpster at once inviting and sickening. Urban decay at its finest. The humans that threw it out there didn't seem to care. Were they just so full that they had no more room in their bellies for more food? Why just dump it out? Why not give it to their fellow humans, some of whom were sitting next to the dogs in the streets asking for food? Even Half-ear and his gang were unreasonable. They could never eat all the food that was dumped out, but they prevented the other dogs from eating it nevertheless. The dog had always had to scrounge for food. It barely remembered its mother. She had been kind. It recalled the warmth and coziness of nuzzling up to her, but when she was hit by the car, he remembered its brothers and sisters lying by her body before going their separate ways. How long ago had that been? It couldn't recall. Time had a strange way of changing a dog's mind. All the dog knew was it had been very hungry ever since. It couldn't remember how it had hurt its leg, it tried hard to think, had it been hit by a car? No, it wasn't that. What was it? Maybe it had been injured in a fight but it couldn't feel any other injuries. Ridiculously it recalled a tree. What did that have to do with it? Anyway, right now it knew it needed to get some food. The dog stealthily stuck to the wall as it approached the alley with the dumpster. If it was lucky the 'The Half-Ear' gang would be asleep. The alley was dark. It could hear the low rumble of conversation from inside the room in front, with the glass windows as people sat eating.

The back door was where the dumpster was; it hoped it had recently been filled and even better that there were no humans around. The dog snuck around the corner and looked around; no other dogs were visible. The fragrance from the dumpster suggested fresh food. The dog's stomach rumbled at the thought. It slowly slunk its way to the dumpster. It saw the barely eaten piece of chicken that had found its way out of the overflowing dumpster and was laying a few feet from it, perfect. The dog quickly scampered over to the dumpster, and darted for the piece of chicken, grabbing it in its mouth and limping away, so far so good. It limped its way to the end of the alley, resisting every impulse in its hungry body to eat the chicken right away. Just because it didn't see the other dogs didn't mean that they weren't far away. As it slowly made its way to the end of the alley, its head low to the ground, its heart stopped, as it heard deep growls that made the hairs on the back of its neck stand up. It looked up to see Half-ear who must've come around the corner to the entrance of the alley with two other dogs flanking it. The dog cowered its head low to the ground. It dropped the piece of chicken lowering his head in submission and whimpering meekly. Hoping against hope that the gang would spare him. It wasn't enough. The dogs attacked with a cacophony of loud barks and terrifying guttural growls. The dog felt a searing pain in its left ear as the dog pounced and yelped loudly, then out of nowhere a loud human voice yelled out, "No!" It felt the splash of cold water on its face startling it. The other dog backed away growling. It couldn't get up. It felt the warm blood from its left ear dripping and the pain from its leg had gotten worse. The dogs had jumped on it and had sunk their teeth into its leg and ripped its ear. The dog was lying in a helpless bundle on the floor unable to get up.

A kind voice said, "He seems to be hurt, Kavita, let's take him to the vet." "Manoj, are you sure? It might bite you if you pick it up, it's a street dog after all."

"It's ok, Kavita, I think it's just a puppy." The man picked up the dog. He looked at it at its ear and leg. "Looks like it's hurt, Kavita! Let's take it to a vet." They put the dog in a blanket that they had gotten from the car.

"It's a good thing I had a bottle of water from the restaurant," said the man they called Manoj. "We need to take it to the vet. Hopefully they're still open." The dog lay in the backseat. Kavita sat next to it comforting it with kind words. The dog whimpered quietly. He liked the two of them instantly or perhaps he just didn't know any better. No human had ever treated it with any kindness. The best it had known prior to this was a man in the park who threw his leftover sandwich in his direction as he walked away. These two seemed genuinely upset by its wounds. The man drove the car for a few minutes before stopping in front of a large building. They found a vet as Manoj had said, the dog had no idea what that meant. They took him out of the car and walked into a white building with bright lights, exactly the kind of place strays like him knew to avoid. The rain was stopping now and became not much more than a drizzle. The cool air felt good on his wounds. As Kavita carried him in, the dog smelled the nastiest smell in the air, a mixture of urine, dog poop, and fear. It whimpered and tried to jump out of Kavita's hands, but she held it firmly saying, "It's OK," in a kind voice. The dog shrank back into the towel. A woman in a white coat came to meet him.

"Oh-oh, looks like we got into some trouble, haven't we?" she said, taking him from Manoj. "I'm afraid he's been hurt; we saw him being attacked by some bigger dogs."

"He didn't get too badly hurt, did he?" said Manoj.

"We separated them as soon as we could." "Doesn't look like it," the doctor assured them. "So, he isn't yours I take it?" said the lady in the white coat.

"No," said Kavita and explained what had happened. "We've had too many strays in Hyderabad," said the lady in the white coat. "Unfortunately, a lot of them die painful deaths under cars or are killed by other dogs."

"I will get him stitched up for you," said the lady. The next thing the dog knew, he was whisked onto a shiny table. He struggled hard, not knowing what was in store for him. All the while, the lady in the coat kept muttering kind words. Another sturdy woman held him down so it could no longer wriggle. It faced a white wall that had pictures of all kinds of animals. The bright white lights were shining into his eyes, almost blinding him. Then suddenly, a firm hand went over its eyes. It tried to struggle and even bite. There was a man firmly holding the dog down and he strapped its mouth. The woman was busy at the table. The dog heard the clinking of objects on the steel table. When she turned, she had an object with a sharp needle at its end. The dog struggled as she approached, but the man was too strong and clearly had done this many times. The dog felt a sharp painful jab in his ear as the needle pierced it. Heat seared through his brain.

He landed on the ground and rolled on impact. As he stood up, he tried to speak but he could not. He looked up and saw an old woman laughing at him. "I hope you didn't hurt yourself! He! He! He!" she cackled. He tried to talk again but was only able to utter some growling sounds. Kautilya sat on the rough ground. He was not hurt too badly. *Who was the decrepit woman?* He thought to himself. *Where was he?* Slowly the fog cleared. He looked around him. There was a large Banyan tree with wide-reaching branches. It was dark and a fire crackled a few feet away with a pot of food bubbling inside. Kautilya! That's who he was. The old hag had made him climb the tree, he remembered. He turned to her angrily. "What's going on? Why did you make me climb the tree?" His voice was more normal now. He remembered he had been very hungry and for some reason, his left ear hurt. He touched it and it was bleeding! How?

Chapter 4

"Sit down for a while, young man," the old woman said. "Eat something, I finished making the khichdi while you were gone."

"Gone? Where?" asked Kautilya.

"Well up the tree," she answered elusively. She glanced at him furtively, as she used a large leaf as a plate and scooped up some khichdi. She handed him the steaming food; the hunger which was forgotten now rose again. He was famished. How long had it been since he had eaten? It felt like forever. Kautilya ate the khichdi and his stomach felt better. As the hunger slowly subsided, he remembered why he had set off from home in the first place. He felt for the small bag at his waist that had the gems in it. They were still there. He heaved a sigh of relief. At least, that part hadn't gone wrong yet. The old woman hadn't robbed him. It was not uncommon for travelers on the road to be drugged with herbs and after being robbed, left wandering in a stupor.

Kautilya looked at the woman. "What is your name?" he asked.

"It depends," she said.

"Depends?" said Kautilya, convinced of her insanity. She had been speaking in riddles since he had met her.

"Yes, it depends on where you are and who you are." "For you, Kautilya, I am Sabari. I was born in Venkatapuram about 1000 kosas from here."

"How old are you?" said Kautilya.

"Old," she said, "I have lost track." A thousand kosas, that's really far!

"How did you get here? It seems like a really long distance to travel for someone your age," said Kautilya.

"I know you have a lot of questions, Kautilya. Sit down, this is going to take some time," said Sabari. Kautilya sat down on a twisted root of the banyan tree that wound sinuously across the ground. Sabari, as the woman called herself, sat down with an odd smile. "All right, who do you think you are right now?" said Sabari.

"I already told you, I am Kautilya from Kalinga. My father is Gautama, his father is Vismaya, my mother is Vaidehi. Do you want me to go on?"

"What if I told you that it doesn't matter where you are from or who you are?" said Sabari.

"What do you mean? Of course, it matters, they make me who I am. My parents, my family, my village," said Kautilya.

"The only thing that matters," said Sabari, "is now! All else is irrelevant. Think of it as a long string of beads that winds through eternity. Each of our lives is a bead, the soul is the string that connects these beads. Does it matter which bead you hold as long as you recognize the soul that runs through them to be the same?" As she kept talking, Kautilya became dizzy. The image of Sabari began to waver in front of his eyes, his eyes began to water. Sabari called out to him "Kautilya! Kautilya!" her voice now changed, Kautilya blinked.

"Amit! Amit!" said Mr Kailash, his deep resonant voice breaking through the fog in Amit's head. "As I was saying, all that matters is the NOW, *this now* could be anywhere," said Mr Kailash. What was happening? Was the woman a witch? or a ghoul who hung from banyan trees that he had always been warned about? Mr Kailash continued, "Oh dear! We must try to get you settled down. Who do you think you are now? Kautilya or Amit?" His head swam. Who was he? He looked around; he was sitting in a small classroom. He knew this place was a classroom at the back of the temple where he had come for his yoga lessons. Mr Kailash was looking old, much older than he remembered. Amit, of course, he was Amit, his mother was Kavita and his father was Manoj.

The confusion in his head dissipated somewhat. Mr Kailash continued to talk. "As I was saying, Amit, if this is you at this moment in time, is it possible that you have other existences?" Mr Kailash continued the conversation as if it had never stopped. The juxtaposition of Mr Kailash and Sabari was jarring, even funny.

"Do you mean like past lives?" asked Amit. The memory of Kautilya began to slowly fade in his brain into a hazy memory, as if he had been a long-lost relative, albeit a close one. Had he really been talking to somebody else, or had he dozed off during the yoga class, and Mr Kailash somehow able to read his dreams?

"Think about this Amit, your soul can be a part of this vehicle that is your body in this time, but have been part of another vehicle in another time. Irrespective of the vehicle the soul is the same." Amit was perplexed. What was Mr Kailash talking about? He needed to go home. He turned to Mr Kailash and said, "I need to get some rest, my head hurts." And before he could reply, Amit ran out of the class. It was sunny and warm outside; it was late afternoon and the sun hit him in his eyes as he tried to look for his car. The warmth of the sun felt good on his skin. It felt like it had been ages since he had breathed fresh air and he took deep breaths trying to calm his mind. What was the color, he couldn't think about what his car looked like! Perplexed, he put his hands in his pocket and felt a bunch of keys. He picked up the key fob and pressed the button, a red Toyota Sienna in the lot chirped and flashed its lights. This was his car! He got inside the car backing out slowly from the spot, driving more carefully than usual. He came out of the lot of the temple and drove home, traffic was light and he continued to think about all the bizarre happenings of the day. What had he done and why was Mr Kailash talking about different lives and realities to him? He recalled with a groan that he had a math assignment due tomorrow.

As he pulled into the driveway of his home, he pressed the garage opener. The garage slowly opened to reveal one other car, a Tesla. When had his dad bought a Tesla? His house looked familiar and yet was different. The landscaping was different. It seemed that there had been quite a few changes since he was last here. He pulled in beside the Tesla and got out of the car. As he opened the garage door, he heard noises inside, indistinct child-like screams of delight could be heard. As he entered the house through the garage door it opened into the kitchen. At the stove, stirring a pot stood a woman. Without turning, she said, "Hi honey! How was your guy's evening out?" Was this his mother? The voice was not hers for sure. She put the ladle down and turned. It was a woman he didn't recognize. Her long curly hair framed a pretty face. She walked over to him and hugged him, as she shouted, "Kids, Nana is here!" The 'kids', a girl around eight and a boy of around six ran to him and they each gave him a big hug, both trying to talk to him simultaneously. What was going on? How? He talked to them briefly, mumbling his responses in monotone, and walked to the bathroom. How did he know where it was in this strange home? He shut the door behind, drowning out the kids, who were talking to him even as he was walking away. He turned on the light and looked in the mirror, startled to see a middle-aged man staring back at him. The Amit in his mind's image of himself had been an 18-year-old boy. The man that stared at him appeared to be around 35 or so. So, this was his wife? These were his children? Who was he? He showered and went down for dinner. He helped set up the dinner plates and let his instinct guide him. He automatically knew where the plates and glasses were kept. The kids continued to chatter around him during their play, oblivious to his bewilderment. As he sat down to eat the spread of the Kura, pappu and rasam that smelt divine, his 'wife' glanced at him during the meal as the kids were telling him about their day and all they had done. She appeared worried but he smiled what he hoped was a reassuring smile at her.

"Just feeling a little tired, that's all," he said in answer to the unasked question in her eyes. She smiled back, "Maybe, you are coming down with something."

"What does that mean - coming down with something?" piped in his son Amar. His name was Amar, it came back to him.

"It just means I am not feeling well," he said.

"Oh no!" Amar said, sadness on his face. "Does that mean we will have to cancel our trip next week?" Their planned trip to Universal Studios had been on his mind for weeks now.

"No, I am sure you will feel better after a good night's sleep," said his daughter, Lakshmi, with a smile. This was an inside line between father and daughter. Amit now recalled that he had always told her that whenever she felt ill. Childhood memories that he didn't have when he entered the house earlier came flooding back to his brain. In his mind's eye, he recalled Lakshmi running up to him with her scraped knee, crying. Amit had replied, "It will get better if you sleep it off." She was initially irritated, anger flashing in her large brown eyes. Then, she laughed it off, and it soon became a thing every time she was hurt. Amit laughed in reply, eating his rasam.

In the night, he lay in bed beside the woman who must've been his wife, thinking, unable to sleep. He stared at the wall opposite the bed. It was colored light green. The bed light he had turned on was just bright enough to catch its color. It was covered with printed pictures the size of tiles. He got up carefully, trying not to wake up Aparna, who was fast asleep next to him. He looked at the pictures of the family on various trips. The kids got older as their pictures progressed across the wall. Little flashes of memory came to him as he saw himself holding a baby Amar, the Eiffel Tower in the background. His head framed halo-like by the lights on the Eiffel Tower. He looked at another of Lakshmi smiling up from the crib, her face filled with delight as she played peek-a-boo with him. He remembered the box for the crib had landed on his foot as he tried to get it up the stairs, leaving a gash on his foot that had left a scar.

A scar the Amit of old did not have. He looked down at his foot and felt the fading scar. As he came upon the radiant face of Aparna with a newborn Lakshmi in her arms, he knew he had to tell her. How much should he tell her? Would she think he was crazy? Heck, he would think he was crazy if he had heard such a story. On the other hand, he needed time. He would need time to sort these things out with Mr Kailash and who knew how long that would certainly take? Not hours in a meditation class at the back of a temple. He woke up his sleeping wife. Aparna woke up with a groggy look on her face. "What? What happened? Are you feeling okay?" she asked, thinking that this had something to do with his feigned illness in the evening.

"I need to talk to you," he said. She saw the seriousness in his face and was worried. "What? What's going on? Something with the kids?" This was just like her. She could be anxious, an understatement, he thought to himself. How would she react when she heard this story? He smiled what he hoped was a reassuring smile.

"No, Aparna, everyone is alive and well, just listen for a bit I will tell you if you don't laugh or promise that you won't call a psychiatrist." She now had a curious expression and sat up wide awake. "This better be worth it!" she said. "Tomorrow is a working day."

Where would he begin? He started telling her about his childhood, the meditation sessions and vivid dreams. He then told her about what had happened to 18-year-old Amit. He told her about Sabari and Mr Kailash. He tried to talk to her about his abilities but he couldn't explain them. He watched as her eyes widened when he told her about the banyan tree. There were big gaps in the story that he couldn't fill. His memories of the dog. He said to her, "I am not sure why this is happening, or even what is actually happening, but I think I have to find out for sure whether this is all in my head or real." Aparna looked at him, her face both shocked and mystified. "Well," he said, "what do you think I should do?"

"Of course there is only one way to know for sure, you idiot!" she said. "Go to Mr Kailash and find out."

"You understand this could take weeks or months, right?" he said.

"I do, but this is something you need to resolve," she said. "Otherwise, you will never be happy or know for sure."

"How do you know I am not just crazy?" asked Amit, looking more for reassurance than anything else.

"One person having a hallucination is one thing but for Mr Kailash to also know the details of those lives definitely means you are not crazy. I will tell the kids you have an international assignment for work." Amit smiled at her, his heart at ease for the first time in hours? Days? Years? This is why he married this woman.

Of course, that's why he needed to go back to Mr Kailash.

As he woke up the next morning, he felt a sinking feeling he would need to break it to the kids that he would be gone for a while. He contemplated what to say as he looked at himself in the mirror. As he brushed, the face that stared back still startled him. Older with just the earliest strands of grey. In the temples, the hairline significantly receded from the Amit he had in his mind's image. He went down the stairs, his heart heavy. He took a deep breath as he sat staring at the kids at the dining table, pausing for a sip of coffee before he began.

"I am going to be gone for a while," he said somewhat abruptly. The kids looked up from their breakfast, startled.

"What about our trip?" said Amar, tears welling up in his large eyes.

"I know, I am sorry. I won't be able to make it. I will be in India for an important assignment. I promise we will go again when I get back. Mommy will take you guys anyway. This was a Monday and a busy day." "When do you leave?" said Lakshmi, always the practical one.

"This afternoon, sorry," Amit said. The kids reluctantly accepted it.

Aparna said, "Don't worry guys, we will have a great time while Nana gets bored on his business trip."

"How lucky that he gets to go to India on a trip while we are stuck here!" said his daughter. "This is so unfair. Why do I have to go to school?"

"You are welcome to go on the trip instead of me and I will go to Universal Studios," said Amit, laughing. Work. He wondered what he did for a living.

As the family slowly left for work and school, the house went quiet. He got off the couch, took a shower, and got dressed. As he sipped the warm coffee, it cleared his brain. He needed to find this Mr Kailash, if that's who that man was, and try to understand how this was happening. How had he, an 18-year-old boy, suddenly acquired a wife and two kids? He let the thought percolate in his mind as he drove to the temple to see if he could find Mr Kailash.

Chapter 5

Mr Kailash was in the temple, sitting at a desk, reading a book. This bald man was also very different from the Mr Kailash he remembered from childhood. He wore jeans and a polo shirt and was bent over his book making him appear so much older than he recalled. He looked up from his book as Amit walked in. He put down his book and his face lit up with relief. He got up and hugged him.

"I'm so glad you came back Amit. I was so worried about you; you must have a million questions. I just wanted to make sure you didn't do anything stupid. Sit down." Amit looked suspiciously at Mr Kailash.

"I will explain everything, but first, you need to try to relax," Mr Kailash said. Mr Kailash brought out a yoga mat and had Amit sit down. "First, I want you to do some deep breathing exercises. Follow along precisely as I say, don't want to lose you again," he said and winked at him. The joke was lost on Amit, who looked at him quizzically as he sat down. Now Amit breathed deeply in and out through the right nostril and then through the left. Amit slowly felt his heart rate and breathing slowing, as calm descended over him.

"You Amit have a capability that most of us have had to work years or even decades to acquire and most never acquire it even if they try for lifetimes. An ability to move between different lives that you've lived past, present and future in a seamless manner. Sometimes you remember more and other times less of the lives you've lived."

Amit sounded stunned and replied, "I'm sorry, I don't quite understand. Where are my parents?"

Mr Kailash heaved a sigh. "I guess it would be easier if you saw for yourself. This is not going to be pleasant."

Amit found himself standing at a bedside in a hospital room. His father lay in the bed. His head was bandaged and he had a tube coming out of his chest as well as his mouth. He heard machines beeping by the hospital bed. His mother sat by the bedside and was crying. What had happened? Kavita looked up at him and she walked over to him. She had bandages on her right arm, which was in a sling. She looked up at Amit and put her hand on his face and said, "It's OK, Amit," and broke down crying. Everything was not OK. He remembered there had been an accident. They had been driving on a rainy night on some country roads and a deer had come out of the field. His father swerved right and hit a tree. Amit had not been there. He had been home finishing a science project when he had gotten the call. The beeping slowly stopped. A crowd of medical people gathered around his father as he and his mother were herded out of the room. The doctor who had been caring for his father came out of the room. From his expression, Amit knew what happened. "I am sorry, we were unable to save him." Amit felt an immense sense of sadness as he broke down crying. Waves of grief flooded over him as he sobbed.

"Amit! Amit!" he heard Mr Kailash's voice as he opened his eyes. He felt his cheek wet; he had been crying. His father's death was still fresh in his mind. Mr Kailash spoke to him calmly, "What do you think happened, Amit?" "That was horrible", said Amit. "My father just died." Mr Kailash looked at him. "Did he?" he asked. "Your soul is merely energy. Do you feel sad when you change your clothes, Amit?" Amit looked at him quizzically. "Let me explain." He took some water from the pitcher and put it in a glass. "Is the water any different now, that it's in a glass rather than a pitcher? No, it's still water. Just like water takes the shape of whatever vessel it is in, so the soul also inhabits whatever body it lives in. When one body gets old and dies, it moves to another and becomes an inalienable part of it till the cycle repeats until it becomes part of the larger cosmic energy. Most of us are unable to remember anything from a previous life, and most are oblivious to any previous existence, just like this water in the glass doesn't know that it was ever in a pitcher. Some on the other hand recognize that time is merely a construct that we have imposed on the soul. That some souls move between times and bodies with the memory of all or at least some of their previous lives. Some of us through meditation have some understanding of this. You, for some reason, seem to be able to do it without much training. The Banyan Tree, we found, is also some sort of a portal that seems to be able to transport you between different lives without any effort. The Banyan tree, the old woman, what was her name?" Of course, Sabari! Kautilya! It all came rushing back to him. How did Mr Kailash know? "I've been trying to help you find yourself," said Mr Kailash. "You were the old woman!" said a startled Amit.

"And the beggar," said Mr Kailash. Of course, he remembered the cold and the rain. The dog and the man he had run away from. Amit was overwhelmed. "Who are you?" Mr Kailash asked again. "I am Amit," he replied, still trying to make sense of it all. "Are you? What if I told you that you are Mrignayani, a princess who ruled over a vast kingdom, Raja Mahendravaram, in south India, just about seven hundred years ago?" Amit's eyes glazed over. He was on an elephant and in a magnificent houdah. He was dressed in an exquisitely embroidered red sari but in his hand was a bow and arrow and at his side a long sword with a ruby-encrusted handle. He was in the midst of a battle! Arrows whizzed by him. Mrignayani aimed her bow and shot off a series of arrows, at a soldier trying to climb her elephant. The man went down with a cry. She was at the forefront of a battle, soldiers and horses milled around her elephant. Her army appeared to be worse for the wear; many soldiers appeared crestfallen and defeated. The enemy, easily identifiable by their horned helmets, seemed too far outnumber her soldiers. There were a lot of dead bodies and dying men around her elephant. Mrignayani saw the king of the Vatsala army Suryavarma about 200 meters away from her. Surveying the damage, he had a smile on his face as he exhorted his men onwards. It had come to this because she had refused to kneel and take him for her husband. The arrogance of this woman. Surya Varma was a brash young prince whom she had known when they were both younger. Their fathers had been friends, the kingdom of Raja Mahendravaram was a powerful kingdom that controlled more than 800 square miles in the south. Vatsala had always had good relations with them for centuries until the old kings of both kingdoms died within months of each other. Mrignayani had received a marriage proposal from Surya Varma. She had politely refused and sent condolences for the death of his father and hoped that the two kingdoms could continue their long friendship and alliance. In reply, Surya Varma sent an ultimatum to marry him or else he would attack. Mrignayani, never one to be cowed down, tried again to make peace, but to no avail. So here they were in the midst of battle. Years of peace and neglect by her father had made her army rusty and ill-prepared for battle, but this was inevitable.

Mrignayani knew what she had to do. She directed her mahout to charge the king's elephant. Her mahout said, "Rani, it's too dangerous! They are too far away and the elephant will be too tired. It'll make you an easy target for their archers and infantrymen."

"Do as I say," said Mrignayani in a steely voice. The mahout goaded the elephant it trumpeted loudly, and charged in the direction of Surya Varma's elephant. He did not notice her initially in the melee of the battle, but as she approached closer, the soldiers guarding him shot at the oncoming elephant. A few even attempted to jump on the elephant and some threw spears at it. The arrows bounced off the elephant's thick leather armor and skin. Mrignayani was loading and shooting arrows at a tremendous pace at the soldiers surrounding Surya Varma. They hit with impeccable precision, piercing their armor and helmets and taking them down. As she got within 10 meters off the Vatsala king's elephant, Mrignayani drew her curved 4-foot sword. Its blade glistened in the sun. Surya Varma stood up, sword drawn, ready to meet her charge.

This was insane, he thought. Well, at least, the battle will come to a swift end. Once I get rid of this annoying woman. She was coming straight at him. *This would be easy,* thought Surya Varma. He was a handsome man, his manicured mustache curled just so. As Mrignayani approached the Vatsala king's elephant, she leaped on its back. He expected a battle in close quarters and stood sword-drawn, ready to meet her. His haughty face was contemptuous. *This was her plan? More like a suicide mission.* She did not attack him directly. Suryaprakash looked surprised as she balanced precariously on the elephant's back, just outside the houdah and out of reach of his sword, and as her sword flashed, he understood too late what she was doing. She slashed the ropes holding the houdah onto the elephant. The houdah tilted precariously as she cut the ropes. When she hit the final rope, it crashed to the ground, taking the king with it. In a trice, she jumped off the elephant and took off the king's head in one smooth motion of her sword. The Vatsala soldiers looked shocked. Before they could regain their senses, she jumped on to her own elephant's trunk which carried her onto its back and into her own houdah. She took out a bugle and blew it loudly. Once her men realized what had happened, they cheered loudly. The cheer spread through the battlefield in a wave. The Vatsala army realized their king was down and now had nothing to fight for. They turned and ran away. The route was completed. The victorious army shouted out their cheers! Jai Mrignayani! Jai Mrignayani!

At this moment in the classroom at the back of the temple, Amit felt his chest swell with pride. He stood tall beaming! Mr Kailash looked at him. He walked to the corner of the room and picked up two samurai swords and threw one at Amit. Without giving him much time to think, ran at him with the other raised high, looking to cut him in half. Amit expertly caught the sword flung at him and blocked the blow that would surely have killed him. The sound of the steely clash rang out against the walls. As he turned, Mr Kailash attacked again. Amit parried, dancing out-of-the-way. The clanging of the katanas rang through the room.

"See Amit," Amit," Mr Kailash said, "you do remember." Amit had images of life and death flash through his mind. The faces and emotions of many different lives and deaths and battles rushed through his brain like a kaleidoscope of images. Tears ran down his face at the immensity of it all. It was like he was on a train. Each compartment was a life with all its memories and emotions and as it hurtled along time, he was able to go from one compartment to the next effortlessly. Like a spiderweb, each strand of life radiated in different directions and he was able to cut across different ones. The moment soon passed. The vision, if he could describe it as such, was soon gone. He became Amit again, completely.

"Is this real? Am I real?" he asked Mr Kailash as he put his hands on his face. "Each life is real, in its own respect, but it is the soul that is eternal," said Mr Kailash. "Are there more people like us? Like you and me?" said Amit. "I don't know," said Mr Kailash. "In the earlier days, Rishis would meditate for years on end and acquire knowledge of their various lives. Some were able to postpone death, even indefinitely. I spent a lot of years with a Guru, who was able to teach me meditation techniques, and soon, I realized that I was able to see and experience different lives and could choose to be anywhere in them. The Guru told me that there was another and led me to you. The Guru wanted me to watch over you and bring you when you were awakened and ready. Now, Amit, our journey begins.

<h1 style="text-align:center">Chapter 6</h1>

Amit and Mr Kailash took the flight to New Delhi from Chicago the next day. The chaos of O'Hare enveloped them. People milled around dragging suitcases and pushing carts. Rude airline staff harried the meek passengers weighing their suitcases to the ounce. Tears rolled down many a cheek as couples and families parted. The plane slowly pulled out onto the runway, its engine revving up. Amit wondered how long he would be gone. Weeks? months? He was unable to provide Aparna with a great answer but said he would be gone for a few weeks and that he would call.

Mr Kailash sat in his seat appearing pensive but with a hint of a smile on his face.

Amit realized that he knew next to nothing about Mr Kailash. "Mr Kailash?" said Amit. He turned to look at him with concern. Amit tried to appear reassuring in his expression, as Mr Kailash had been worried about him. "Mr Kailash, how did you end up teaching yoga at the temple? I heard you had gone to an ashram, was it the same one we are going to? What prompted you to do this? I realize I barely know anything about you and with all the traveling I have been doing, I haven't had a chance to find out," said Amit with a smile.

Mr Kailash's face had a wistful smile. It was a smile mixed with pain. Mr Kailash stared for a few moments, watching the passing clouds. "Amit, there was a time when I was career-driven, motivated. You know, the American dream and all that. I was always trying to publish and worked myself to the goal of becoming a Professor. All that changed one night when I received the news. I had just dropped my wife Anjali and baby son Sunil at the airport. They were going to India on his first trip. He was just about to turn a year old and we wanted to celebrate his birthday in India, like a lot of Indian parents. I couldn't leave with them, I had to submit my paper to make the publication deadline and was going to join them the following week. I turned on the radio on the way home, settling in for the hour drive from O'Hare airport to Valparaiso. That's when I heard it on the news. The plane had crashed on take-off, killing all passengers. It ended my life, as I knew it, at that moment. Nothing mattered anymore, not my career, not my life. As you can imagine, I fell into a deep depression. I questioned everything that I knew about life and religion. Why would God do such a thing? The awfulness of it overwhelmed me and I did nothing for months, just existing. Then one of my good friends forced me on a plane to India to the very ashram that we are going to. There I understood that a soul's journey is endless until Nirvana and that my wife and son had merely changed vehicles. That I would forever be a part of their soul, and they of mine. Life took on a different meaning and I worked with the guru to gain some understanding and with that understanding, some skills."

Amit's eyes welled over. He had not heard this part of the story from anyone before. Mr Kailash was truly unique. "The Guru that you worked with, what's his name?" asked Amit. "Her name is Vrinda," he said.

As Amit and Mr Kailash waited for the flight to Srinagar at Delhi airport. Announcements rang out loudly over the cacophony of chattering people and crying children. The ding of the overhead system each time an announcement was made was jarring. In a strange way, the airport seemed to embody all he had heard over the last few days. *The chaos of life itself,* Amit thought. He was still absorbing all that had happened. What was he doing? All he knew for sure was that he could understand things and experience things that clearly others didn't. If he had any doubts on this count, they were removed the moment at the temple when he seemed to embody all his lived lives at once. Clearly, this didn't happen to everybody. He was disappointed that he was unable to hold onto that moment of clarity forever. As it faded in his mind, doubts came back. The doubts about Amit. They were very quiet on the flight to Srinagar. Mr Kailash looked out the window pensively. Amit sat, trying to read a book, but was unable to get his mind into it. They landed in Srinagar and got their bags. As they stepped out into the cold air and the chaos of the sidewalk, a taxi drove up. A tall man with a scraggly beard and worn brown shirt stepped out clearly recognizing Mr Kailash. As they put their bags in the trunk of the beat-up white ambassador car, Mr Kailash explained that he had set up the taxi from the airport to the lower Himalayan village where the guru lived. They drove through the beautiful lower Himalayan landscape in Kashmir. There was a fragrance of pine in the air. The skies outside slowly darkened as the evening wore on. The drive in the mountains was slow and the roads were treacherous. Landslides were extremely common around here, especially after the rains, and the evidence of prior landslides was everywhere.

It was late October and the snow had not yet started, except in the highest reaches of the mountains. They reached a small village surrounded by the snowy foothills of the Himalayas. "This is the town of Ransi," said Mr Kailash. The Rishi has had her Ashram here for several decades. They drove into a somewhat dusty village that consisted of nothing more than a few dozen houses around the muddy road; there were maybe another 30-40 houses reaching up the hillsides. At the end of the village was a large compound surrounded by a low rock wall with moss growing on it. It was the largest structure in the little village. As they drove into the compound through a wrought-iron gate, Amit noticed that it consisted of about 10 or 12 huts that surrounded a larger central enclosure. The houses were mostly constructed of pinewood with slanting roofs. The wood itself was weather-worn.

As he stepped out of the car, he noticed it was bitterly cold with a biting wind. The taxi had stopped in front of a small cabin. Mr Kailash, having obviously been here before, began to take out the bags from the trunk. Amit stepped out of the taxi, looking around him, taking in the surroundings. He then walked to the back of the car to help move their bags into the cabin. It was sparsely furnished with two small cots that lay by each of the sidewalls of the room; the other wall had an empty wooden cupboard. The bathroom was a common one for several of the cabins and it did involve walking in the bitter cold.

After they unpacked their clothes, Amit braved a trip to the bathroom. The cold was like nothing he had felt before. The lack of heating was not something he had experienced before. *At least in this life,* he smiled to himself at the thought. When he returned from the bathroom, he and Mr Kailash walked to the bathroom to the central enclosure and entered through a side door, into a room that was clearly a central dining space which was empty at this time. Mr Kailash walked in and was recognized by an older white gentleman in the back with a scraggly beard. He wore a simple kurta and a thick woolen shawl over it. "Hi Kailash, it's been a while!" and they both shook hands and smiled. "We have some upma if you guys are hungry and some yogurt and fruit."

"That sounds perfect," said Mr Kailash. The warm upma was perfect for the weather.

Amit walked back to the room as Mr Kailash stayed to catch up with Tom, which was the name he introduced himself with. Tom had apparently been a Wall Street type who had grown dissatisfied with his life and had eventually stumbled upon the ashram over 10 years ago. He functioned as the cook and pantry manager. He explained to Amit that they all had jobs that they chose or were assigned and that about 30 other sadhus lived in the ashram. Mr Kailash and Tom caught up. They had known each other for a while apparently. Mr Kailash told him he looked exhausted and suggested he head back to the room. Amit was more than happy to oblige. The flight had been long and the drive was bumpy and so, he decided to go to his room as the jet lag caught up with him.

He changed and lay down on the cold bed. He shivered as he pulled the rough blankets over him. He hoped he had enough warm clothes. Thoughts of the last few days ran through his mind. Days, he smiled to himself. All that had happened had him questioning what that even meant.

Chapter 7

Amit was shaken awake by Mr Kailash. It felt like he had barely fallen asleep. "Go take a bath, Amit, and get dressed. We have to meet the guru in half an hour." "What time is it?" he asked.

"It's 5," said Mr Kailash. "A bath! In this temperature?" Amit shivered as he got out of bed and walked to the common bathroom. The cold water jolted his body but later it filled his skin with the sensation of a warm tingling as he put on his clothes. Mr Kailash was already dressed and waiting for him in his room. Amit was a little nervous. Was he really who they thought he was? Or was it all just in his crazy mind? He walked pensively to the large central cabin. As he entered, he saw a middle-aged woman surrounded by about four or five men and a few other women. She had her eyes closed in meditation. She wore a simple hand-woven sari that was a faded white and appeared like any other middle-aged woman in India. She had a large red bindi on her forehead. Amit was somewhat surprised and perhaps a little disappointed. Was this the Guru? Mr Kailash sat down at the back of the room and Amit sat next to him. Mr Kailash closed his eyes in meditation, joining the group. Amit, unsure as to what he was doing, followed suit. "Om... Om..." chanted the group. Amit felt his breathing slow down as he started drifting away. This time, he felt merely unmoored from his body, surrounded by blackness, as if floating in space. It was a lightness of being that felt very comforting. Soon, the thoughts of Amit's present self disappeared as he just floated. He was aroused from this state by a sense of somebody calling him. This was a voiceless call as if somebody had spoken directly into his mind. "I see that you've at least been able to control yourself to the extent that you're not hurtling from one life to the other," the voice said. Amit looked at the other person in front of him also floating in the void. It was the guru!

"I assumed the body you know me by Amit," she said. "Otherwise here we are shapeless, voiceless. What do you want from me, Amit?" she said. "Mr Kailash thought that you might be able to help me," he answered.

"You didn't answer my question, Amit. What do you want from me?" she said.

The question echoed in Amit's mind: *What did he want?* "I feel like I'm the way I am, for a reason, a purpose," said Amit. "I want to know why I can do what I can do and what it's meant for."

"Amit, the purpose of your powers and what it is meant for will be apparent to you when the moment comes. What I can do is help you control it so that when the moment comes you will be prepared."

"Can this power be controlled or is there some randomness to it?"

"The fact that you're here in this space is proof itself, Amit," said the Guru. "If you had not been able to meet me here, I would've concluded that this was perhaps a chance or happenstance. How does a boy Kautilya remember another Amit? How does Amit move between different phases of his life?"

"If you had not been able to actually come to this place, I would've thought that this was perhaps more to do with the accidental entanglement, like lives that had crossed over time, rather than something to do with you."

"What about the Banyan tree?" asked Amit. "The place where I first made the jump to another life." "The Banyan tree appears to be some sort of a portal between your lives and perhaps others, but I can assure you that it certainly isn't as easy without the Banyan tree. It appears *now* that you don't need the Banyan tree. When your powers were unawakened, perhaps, you did need it."

"Are there others like me? Mr Kailash appears to be able to go between different lives," said Amit. "Yes, there are Rishis and Sadhus who, like Kailash, have worked hard to acquire the skills. But every time they do that, they use up some of the cosmic powers they acquired and become weaker, making it harder for them to move from one life to another easily all the time."

"As far as what Kailash has told me, you seem to move far more effortlessly than I have seen or heard of ever," she said.

Amit slowly faded out of his trance and found the voice of the guru also fading away. He found himself seated alone. In the hut, the other people were long gone. The sun was shining brightly outside. He felt exhausted and hungry and stepped out of the hut into the biting cold but the bright midday sun. He walked back to his hut and found Mr Kailash sitting on his bed reading a book. "How did it go?" he asked.

"It went well," said Amit.

Chapter 8

As Mata Vrinda settled down to her morning meditation, she had a sense of strange foreboding. She knew better than to question such feelings. *Often, the answers followed in due course,* she thought. She let the sensation wash over her. As her eyes closed and she sank into a meditative state, she witnessed in front of her an epic battle. Or rather, the end of an epic battle. Scores of bodies lay strewn on a vast battlefield. Where was this? She had seen battlefields in her visions in the past, but this was exceptionally gruesome; the sheer number of bodies was astounding. Something else was amiss. She initially didn't understand, but as she surveyed the scene, it came to her in a flash. All the bodies belonged to one side! There were hardly any soldiers from the other side. Loud cheers rose from one end of the battlefield. A king was being cheered loudly; his face contorted in a grotesque sneer. One that combined disdain for the dead that lay strewn around him, as well as what could only be described as immeasurable glee at their fate.

One of the men, perhaps his commander-in-chief by the sign of his clothes, said, "Sire, they had surrendered! We could have exiled them or taken them prisoner."

The king turned to the commander, his eyes gleaming with anger, and said, "Looks like it's time for me to get a new commander-in-chief. One who reflects my wishes rather than his own." To Mata Vrinda's astonishment, he pulled out what was surely a gun and shot the commander in the chest, killing him instantly. How? Surely, they didn't have any guns during this time.

The image of the battle faded. In her mind's eye, she saw the countryside ravaged by war and the resultant famines. The King's murderous nature had only emboldened the zamindars and local chiefs who ruled the country with savage brutality. Their only rule appeared to be making sure the King received his dues on time. The people were merely instruments for the King to amass more gold in his coffers. Gold was used to arm larger armies to conquer and destroy vast parts of the country.

Mata Vrinda awoke startled from her meditation. What was the meaning of this? She had not seen these visions before. How did the King and his army have all these guns and cannons, so much before anybody else in the world? She knew better than to push for answers. *It would become apparent soon enough,* she told herself.

Chapter 9

The next few days were anything but easy. He did eventually get used to the cold morning bath. It certainly got the brain awake. The ashram was surrounded by gorgeous views of the Himalayan peaks covered with snow. He often was awake early enough to catch the golden light of dawn as the first rays came over the mountains. It was a sight to behold. The morning air was cold and sharp in his nostrils as he breathed in deep, on his way to the central hut where he met with the Guru every morning. She usually just smiled in greeting, not saying much at all. Her smile, though, was extremely comforting, gently spreading across her face and seeming to radiate warmth. The red bottu on her forehead was transfixing. She always dressed in simple cotton saris that were homespun, usually in dull shades of beige.

Mr Kailash accompanied him to these morning sessions and usually sat quietly watching as the Guru and Amit sat in meditation. Initially, the guru had him recite simple mantras for meditation. The first time he sat down to it, he found himself slowly drifting away. The air around him became warmer and as his eyes opened, he looked upon the ocean with thunderous waves crashing upon a rocky beach. The waves were enormous and he could see surfers riding them, heard sounds of laughing, screaming children surrounding him. Suddenly he felt a force pulling him as though grabbing his arms and drawing him into a bright light in the sky. He was startled awake and found himself back at the ashram.

The guru said to him, "You see how your mind wanders? You cannot let your mind drag you without control into different lives. You need to practice to be able to control your mind and ultimately that control will give you the freedom to wander at will and avoid being dragged away by the impulse of each separate life. Dhyana is the practice of this. Repeat the mantra again and again, and if you wander off into another life, you must be able to pull it back to this one." The challenge of his new life was becoming apparent to Amit. It was difficult; every time he got deeper into meditation his mind apparently became drawn to another life and pulled him into different bodies. Over the next few days, he was a bushman in Africa, an antelope running through a forest in India, trying to escape a hunter's arrow. Several times, the Guru herself had to pull him back to the present using her own powers.

Slowly he was able to do better and better. Each time a life beckoned, he was seemingly able to hover over his own being in that life. He was within and without the bushman as he hunted. He was able to observe. As he crouched amidst an arid landscape surrounded by dry shrub trees, he felt the dry air in his nostrils, the smell of the prey he was tracking. The warmth of the sun beating down on his back, a warmth that reached him in the cold room in the ashram.

The guru made him do this repeatedly, until he had been to so many of his previous existences that the present began to blur. Three months had passed and the Guru became more convinced that he had finally started the process to master his abilities and move between lives without either becoming attached or drawn into the lives he visited.

One day, the guru said, "It is now time to focus on Dharana, a complete immersion with obliviousness to your surroundings, focusing only on the object of your attention." She smiled at him, eyes crinkling with mischief. "Do you think you'll be able to handle this without becoming a dog?" Amit laughed. "I hope so, otherwise Mr Kailash will have to come to rescue me again." Dharana was difficult, it required Amit to hold his mind on one particular object and then be thoughtless—that is, without any other thought wandering into his mind. He also had to be oblivious of any other input from his other senses. He found himself distracted by the slightest noise, sometimes he would have a tremendous urge to scratch his thigh. On another, the ticking of the clock on the wall would appear to grow louder and louder until it seemed to sound like a cannon. Months passed and his concentration gradually improved.

He sat in the meditation hall one early afternoon, trying to work on his concentration when it was broken by the sound of a loud thumping and vibrations. Startled, he opened his eyes to find himself surrounded by four large 5-foot speakers from which the thumping bass of 'Let's Get It Started' by the Black Eyed Peas pulsated. *What was going on?*

In the corner of the room, the Guru and Mr Kailash were laughing loudly. They had planned it! "Is that all it takes?" said the Guru, "a few speakers to get your attention."

Amit was shocked, but couldn't help bursting out laughing. The song was so incongruous to the setting that it was hilarious. As they laughed together, Amit and the Guru sat down.

"Amit, you must've heard the story of Arjuna and the eye of the bird?" "Only a few hundred times," replied Amit.

"Let's go over it again," she said. "Legend has it that Arjuna and the other Pandavas and the Kauravas were put to a test by Drona, their Guru. They were asked to shoot an arrow at a wooden bird suspended high on a tree. Each Kaurava walked up confidently and failed to hit the bird. Then came the turn of the Pandavas. They too failed one by one. Then came Arjuna's turn. He walked up, drew his bow, and stared at the bird, and released the arrow. He then walked off not bothering to look to see if he had hit the bird, and of course, his arrow was unerring and pierced the wooden bird in its eye. Drona then asked each of the Kauravas and then the Pandavas what they saw as they aimed. They described the tree, the branches, the color of the bird, etc. Drona then asked Arjuna what he saw. "The eye," he replied. "What color was the bird?" Drona asked. "I don't know," said Arjuna. "I had to hit the eye and I saw the eye." "Clearly," said the Guru to Amit, "your mind is still distracted by all the other senses and has not reached that point yet. And you will only be able to achieve control when you can control the senses."

Chapter 10

Outside it was summer. The hills that surrounded the ashram were covered in blue wildflowers. The valleys had waterfalls cascading down from the snowmelt. Amit decided to take a walk. He had grown lean over the last 4 months that he had been at the ashram but felt stronger than ever. The sun was bright, the higher peaks with snow seemed to glimmer in the clear sunshine. Wildflowers were fragrant as he made his way up the mountain. The sound of his footsteps was all he heard. The crunch of gravel under his feet was almost hypnotic. Halfway up, he tried to catch his breath while sitting on a rock. He was breathing a little heavier and the thin mountain air made it hard to breathe easily. He had mostly gotten used to the high altitude over the last few months, but the slope was steeper than he expected. He tried to observe his breath going in and out, slowly getting into a deeper meditative state. The chirping of the birds was all he heard, the rhythmic 'Cheep! Cheep! Cheep!' was all that was in his mind, until even that seemed to disappear. He was again floating in nothingness; he felt the calm of the void. Just like that, he seemed to understand it! It was like learning to ride a bicycle, the moment he was suddenly able to ride without putting his legs on the ground or falling. For all the times he had fallen off the bike, once he had the balance, there didn't appear to be a time when he didn't know how to do it. Amit heard a familiar voice calling his name. This time, it was disembodied, yet in his head, and at that moment, he understood. Something seemed to turn on in his head. The truth became apparent.

The voice conveyed to him wordlessly, "Remember this feeling, Amit. The balance. The balance between thoughts and control. The power to shut down your senses and turn on only your mind. Remember this calm. Remember the path you took to get here."

As he descended the mountain, he was elated, a lightness enveloped his soul. When he returned to the ashram, he saw the other Sadhus tending to the garden in the late afternoon sun. Amit smiled and waved at them. He walked into the meditation hall. The Guru was sitting, talking to Mr Kailash. As she looked up at him, she seemed to understand. She asked him, "Ready?" "Yes!" said Amit with determination. He walked to the mat opposite the Guru and sat down. He closed his eyes, breathing slowly, immediately sinking into a deep meditative state. As Amit sat there, breathing slower and deeper with each breath, he became completely oblivious to everything around him, his body simply floating in nothingness. Meanwhile, the guru had plans of her own.

She sent word to all the members of the ashram and had them gather in the meditation hall. They brought every manner of musical instrument. There were six guitars, four sets of tablas, and three harmonium sets. The group talked loudly around Amit, as they set up their instruments and decided what to play. Song after song was played initially. They played without microphones, then the Guru had them bring in microphones and attach them to the large speakers previously set up, the volume turned up too high.

They played the loudest songs they could think of. Their lack of practice and skills made them a cacophonous bunch. The ashram's wooden beams and thatched roof vibrated with the din. Amit sat, serene, breathing in and out, rhythmically unperturbed. When the music failed to move Amit, the guru asked for stoves to be bought in and had the cook make some sambhar, Amit's favorite food, right next to him. The smell of sambhar wafted through the entire meditation hall. Amit still remained unmoved. Then the other sadhus were dispatched to use their imagination to distract Amit. A few minutes later, they returned. Some brought back stink bugs. A few others found some rafflesia flowers. The powerful odor of the flower was famously awful, smelling of dead carcasses. The sadhus crushed the bugs and the flowers near Amit. The odor was overpowering. Some of the Sadhus were nauseated and had to throw up. Amit still sat on. Finally, the Guru asked for a bucket of ice water and the gathered Sadhus wondered what she was up to. She then took Amit's hand and put it in. A few of them gasped, but Amit did not flinch. Everyone's eyes turned to the clock on the wall as the second hand slowly made its way around. Everyone in the room watched Amit's face with rapt attention. Would he flinch? A minute passed, absolutely nothing, and then a second. The ticking of the clock rang through the room in the silence. At five minutes the Guru took out Amit's hand out of the water and wrapped it in a warm towel. Amit's hand, as it came out of the freezing water, was white and wrinkly. The Guru then turned to look at the Sadhus. "Let's leave him," she said. She beckoned to Mr Kailash and said, "You stay and watch." As the light outside the meditation hall was fading in the setting sun, soon Mr Kailash had to go and turn on the lights as the room became darker and darker. At about 8, the Guru came back with some food for Mr Kailash and told him to go to his room and get some rest. He agreed somewhat reluctantly. The Guru looked at Amit. His expression was serene. It had been eight hours!

Chapter 11

Amit felt a sense of nothingness around him. It was like his mind was floating in Jell-O. The darkness was all-encompassing, it seemed to penetrate his body, except it was like he did not truly have a body. He couldn't recall what he looked like or who he was. Here, he was just a nameless bodiless soul, just existing. Time and physical boundaries did not exist; there was no wind, no sound, no feeling. It was as if none of his senses existed.

After floating in this space for a while, he slowly noticed windows or mirrors that seemed to lead from the darkness with what looked like screens flickering with images at the end of each. It was like he was looking from a great distance through a window, into the neighbors' living room, with images flickering at the end of the windows, except there were hundreds or maybe even thousands of these windows. They surrounded him. They seemed close, yet a great distance away, like you were seeing a disco ball but from the inside. All of the screens and windows were seemingly connected to him, and with little to no effort, Amit was able to travel and peer through these windows. There was no true movement; with just a beginning of thought, he could look into these windows and observe the goings-on impartially. He felt no actual feeling, but he somehow knew that these various windows were connected to him. He looked into one where a man was climbing a mountain. He appeared to be a rock climber. He expertly used his climbing equipment as he made his way up the rocky face.

The snow was falling but the man seemed determined, and oblivious to the weather. The man swung his pickaxe and used his feet to clamber up the rock face, going from one rocky prominence to another expertly. As Amit watched, the man suddenly lost his foothold as he tried to jump from one rocky prominence to another, and fell! Surely to his death? As he fell, he seemed to look right at Amit. Amit felt no feelings. The man had a knowing look in his light brown eyes as he fell thousands of feet. Through another such window, Amit saw a little girl of around 10 years, with dark hair and a black formal dress, playing piano with tremendous skill. She was on stage in front of a large audience. The soundless music reaches Amit. Chopin! Amit watched emotionlessly as her fingers flew across the keys, almost invisible as she hit the notes. After she finished the piece, she turned to the audience and took a bow and the audience of hundreds clapped. She then sat back down and started the next piece. She turned and looked right at Amit.

Not all were as accomplished. Amit looked through one window where there was a bullfight. The bull was huge.

It's glistening black hide had a few gashes where the blood flowed freely, the redness of the blood contrasting against the blackness of its hide. The bull had eyes that were enraged. It stumbled and got up, making a final charge at the Matador. The Matador was bedecked in a white sequin jacket and had white gloves and a ceremonial dagger. In his other hand, a red cape was draped over his arm. As the bull charged, the Matador expertly distracted it with his cape and sidestepped, while stabbing the dagger into the bull's neck. It was now bleeding profusely and sank to its knees, it tried in vain to get up but slowly collapsed. Its breathing was heavy and the light in its eyes slowly faded away as it looked at Amit. He didn't know how long he was in this state, the peace and calm that he felt were immensely comforting. He recalled at the back of his consciousness, in the recesses of his mind, the Guru and the ashram, and turned to go back. The windows faded away and he was back in the darkness. Just like a train leaving a really long tunnel, his mind slowly began to make it out into the light. He recalled his parents, the present, his wife and his children, Mr Kailash and the mountains.

Amit's life became clearer and clearer. He slowly opened his eyes. He saw the Guru sleeping on a rough mattress on the ground next to him. How long had he been gone? As he stirred, she opened her eyes with concern. "Amit... Amit, how are you? Are you alright?" she asked. "Yes," he replied and smiled. For some reason, his left hand felt cold and ached. "What time is it?" he asked. "It's 4 AM and you've been gone for 14 hours," said the Guru. "I am hungry," said Amit. "I'm sure you are," said the Guru as she smiled and hugged him.

Chapter 12

Ugrasena ran! His heart was pounding. Sweat poured down his forehead as the heat sunburned his cheeks. He had on a light chain and leather armor, but even this was too much in the afternoon sun. This would've exhausted another man but he was used to it. He was a mercenary who had traded his loyalties many times. A formidable swordsman who could be bought by the highest bidder. On this occasion, he had double-crossed the Koshala army and had instead made a deal with the ruler of Kalinga. He had warned them of an impending attack and they had walked into a massacre. He was paid well for his services. As a result, he now found himself being chased into the forest. His horse had taken some arrows and had fallen a few miles away, the exhaustion and bleeding finally getting the better of it. As it buckled, Ugrasena had been thrown off the horse but fortunately had not hurt himself. He thought he might have given the soldiers the slip, but they were hot on his heels. He guessed that he was somewhere between the kingdoms of Koshala and Kalinga. This was a particularly desolate stretch, the road now narrowing to a small path in the woods. Hopefully they would soon tire of the chase and give up. He continued to run, trying to keep going till he got some distance between him and the soldiers. They had horses so he was already at a disadvantage. His mouth was parched, but he had to go on. Hopefully, he would come to a stream soon. He crossed a narrow bridge over a dry stream. He had never been this way before and soon came upon an old stone arch. The top of the arch was broken, several large stones that adorned the top surrounded its base where they had fallen. The stones had turned a mossy green and the overgrown shrubs almost surrounded the fallen stones. The roots of a tree ran through the base of the arch and it tilted precariously. It probably commemorated some ancient victory. The Prakrit inscription on its sides was worn down with time. Ugrasena was exhausted. He probably had enough distance between himself and the soldiers so maybe he could stop and rest for a while.

He approached a large banyan tree in a clearing in the forest. It was sunset and the shadows of its branches covered the forest floor. At its base was a small fire and a pot balanced on stones. The fire crackled. Ugrasena drew his sword and stepped cautiously into the clearing. He announced himself loudly that he didn't want to surprise anyone. He was easily capable of dealing with whatever threat came to him, but he was too tired to fight now. In any event, he was just a traveler, he remembered. What did he have to hide? Hearing no one, Ugrasena walked to the pot. The smell of rice and dal was inviting. He was ravenous, the last time he had eaten was the previous night in the village inn. He had nothing to eat all day, having spent a sleepless night in a dungeon. He had not had any food since the idlis from earlier in the day, now long gone from his stomach.

"Anyone here?" he asked again. He peered cautiously around the banyan tree. He kept the trunk to his back so that he would not be attacked from behind. This was an area known to be infested with bandits and he knew any traveler would be wary and armed. He really didn't want to get into a fight at this time. He was starving, and all he could think of was the pot of khichdi. As he rounded the tree, he heard a low growl and he saw a dog glowering at him. Its teeth bared. What was a dog doing here? Was it a stray? It appeared to have a colorful band around its neck. Was it lost? Where was its master? Finally, from behind a low bush, appeared an old hag, doubled over on a crooked stick.

"Who's there?" she asked. She was looking straight at him but did not appear to see him. *She was blind!* Ugrasena became even more alert; she surely had someone with her. "Kautilya, is that you?" she said, tapping her stick and making her way to him. "No, this is Ugrasena" he said. "Who is Kautilya?" he asked suspiciously. Maybe the woman was a decoy while her accomplice attacked from behind. He looked around again, his sword held ready. The old woman hesitated for just a second, "He is the dog, his name is Kautilya."

"Yes, my dog Kautilya, do you not see him? Are you blind?" she said and cackled loudly, her own joke amusing her immensely.

"Yes, I see the mutt," said Ugrasena as he eyed the growling dog. "You better calm him down. He doesn't seem to like me," he said angrily.

"He is just surprised," she said. "Would you like to join me for some food? I was just making dinner," she said as she tapped her way with a stick to the fire. She smiled a slight smile. Ugrasena was still very suspicious. "What are you doing alone in the jungle, so far from civilization?" he asked. "I'm not alone, I have the dog," she said. She seems crazy *but not dangerous,* thought Ugrasena.

"Do you have any water?" he asked her. "I have some," she replied, reaching for a small sack on her back and producing a small gourd. "It's all I have, so don't drink it all."

"Right!" said Ugrasena sneeringly, as he put his mouth to the gourd and drained it to the last drop. He shoved the empty gourd back into her hands and she looked disappointed. He turned to the pot, and using some leaves to protect his hands, he took it off the fire. It appeared to be done. He didn't bother asking the old woman if she wanted any food and proceeded to finish the entire pot. He was hungry. This old hag would have to be dealt with; she would be able to tell the soldiers which way he had gone. Though blind, she appeared to be able to hear and navigate quite well.

As Ugrasena contemplated his next move, he heard the neighing of a horse in the distance. He thought he had misheard. He then paid close attention to the sound, as the breeze rustled through the forest leaves. And there it was again, there was no doubt. He quickly assessed the situation; there was only one path leading into the clearing and one path leading out. The banyan tree stood in the center of the clearing, fanning out to cover a large area. The path led to Kosala. Soon, he heard several horses neighing and the low murmur of distant conversations. There was no doubt it was the soldiers, they had to be headed this way. He did not have any time, he needed to hide. What about the old woman? Soon he heard soldiers' voices arguing amongst themselves. If he ran, they would surely catch up with him. He looked around and realized the only safe hiding place he had was in the banyan tree and all he could hope for was that they do not decide to spend the night here.

As he headed to the tree, the old woman stood in his way. "Stop!" she said. "Get out of my way, you old hag!" shouted Ugrasena. The blind woman stumbled onto his path as he tried to run to the tree. He shoved her out of the way and she fell backward, hitting her head on a large rock. The rock slowly began to be bathed in blood. It seemed to be coming from the gash in the woman's head. She lay very still, she appeared dead. Ugrasena did not give her a second thought. He quickly pulled her body into some bushes so she wouldn't be seen. He then turned and quickly ran to the banyan tree. He needed to get out of sight. His legs just disappeared up into the tree canopy as the convoy of soldiers rolled into the clearing. He climbed up the tree. Its rough bark scraped his skin. He climbed faster and tried to pull himself higher. It had been a very long time since he had climbed a tree. The long chase had exhausted the soldiers, they had not anticipated spending the night in the forest.

"We can catch up to him in the morning," said one of the soldiers. "He has to stop and rest too, and we know he doesn't have a horse," said another snickering.

"No water and no food and no horse, how far can he get?" said another, and the other soldiers nodded. The voices faded as Ugrasena climbed higher. The darkness was getting deeper, it was becoming harder to see. The forest noises with the crickets and frogs soon became a cacophony, helping to hide the sounds from Ugrasena's attempts to climb higher.

The birds were making quite a din. He wanted to get high enough in the tree where he would be comfortable. He likely would have to stay the entire night. He was glad that he had been able to get some food in. He hoped the soldiers would not notice the hastily put-out fire. He needed to get to a place where he wouldn't be heard by the soldiers. He also needed to get there before they settled under the tree and heard him rustling above. As he scrambled up, he saw a spot on the third branch which appeared to be ideal, wide enough as well, with enough foliage to make him almost invisible from the ground. He pulled his way up to the branch. Just a few minutes more and he would be safe. As he reached out to pull himself onto the branch, his foot slipped! He fell! Surely, to his death, either from the fall or at the hand of the soldiers below. The fall was a lot longer than he imagined, the blackness enveloped him. Comforting yet endless. Was he already dead? The darkness seeped into his very brain.

"Bob! Bob!" he heard. What was a Bob? The shouting appeared to be from a man in front of him. It was as if the light had suddenly come on. Ugrasena was startled to find himself in front of a somewhat unkempt man with a run-down leather jacket and a scraggly beard.

"What are you doing, Bob? Are you drunk? Do you wanna make the deal or not?" said the man. He had a shifty look on his face. "Ok! all right, I'll give a $1000, no questions asked," he said with resignation.

"Fine! One thousand dollars it is," he heard himself saying, much to Ugrasena's surprise. What was this language he had spoken? The words were coming out of his mouth but he had no control or understanding of its content. The man called Bob smiled. He watched as the man took out a wad of notes and counted them with grubby hands.

He counted one thousand dollars and gave the money to Bob. "And you are sure it will not be traced back to me, right?" "You have my guarantee," said Bob. After the customer left, Bob looked around and locked the store. He turned the cardboard sign to 'closed'. He took care to lock the deadbolts on the door before he pulled it shut. He had looked around before closing the door, making sure nobody was lurking outside. He pulled on the door twice to make sure it was closed. He didn't need a disgruntled customer trying to come back in for a refund, or worse, the cops. The grungy street outside was under the elevated railroad track. There was trash flying in the street. Stores had flashing signs advertising locksmiths and liquor. Bob had a headache for some reason. He did not feel like himself. What happened a few minutes ago? Everything was fuzzy. The last thing he could recall was a man yelling his name. He went back to the TV monitor in the security room which was recording the transactions in the store. He turned back the tape to about a half-hour or so. There he was, just cleaning a few guns, nothing out of the ordinary. The funny thing was he couldn't recall any of it! There was the man who had just left, he was talking to Bob. He saw him asking for a pistol that could be easily concealed. Clearly, the man himself was not an outstanding citizen of society. The man looked around furtively before getting out his wallet. As he watched himself haggling with the man, Bob suddenly watched his face go blank mid-sentence and noticed 'himself' on the screen just staring into space. The man just kept talking, initially oblivious, but eventually, he looked up and saw Bob staring, appearing completely out of it. He waved his hands in front of him and began to yell at him. This was the point from which he remembered. Did he have a seizure? Bob went back to the small room in the back of the store where he had a bed and a little kitchenette and had spent the last 10 years. He laid down and closed his eyes. As he slowly dozed off, it came back to him. Ugrasena! He remembered the soldiers and how they were chasing him! He remembered his life as Ugrasena. Who was he now? Was he dreaming of Ugrasena or was Bob dreaming of Ugrasena? He decided to get some sleep and see if this made any more sense in the morning.

Chapter 13

He had a restless night interrupted by visions of soldiers and an old woman. The woman in his dreams, if that's what they were, appeared to be looking straight at him. For a man who had never been out of the country, his dreams contained images of large forts and trumpeting elephants in battles. The pungent smell of blood and sweat was all around him as men fell in a medieval battle. Bob got up with a cold sweat, his legs were tired as though he had been running for hours. He still had Ugrasena clearly in his head. *This appears to be some sort of an alternate dimension or other reality,* he thought. It was like he had watched too much of the *Twilight Zone* or the *X Files*, both shows he loved. Who could he talk to about this? *No one!* He answered to himself. They would think that he was crazy. All that would result in is being taken to the hospital and then seeing a psychiatrist. Much as he tried, he couldn't forget the image of Ugrasena. The images and memories were so foreign and unreal, yet felt as real as any other event in his life. He opened the store at around noon, as usual, as no one looking to buy a gun, especially at his store, would ever be up before that. The front of the store had a grill that protected the windows and a closed-circuit camera that monitored the door.

The dust hung heavy over all corners of the store. Boxes of ammunition and cartons of guns lined the entry, creating a sort of passageway. The grime of the street mixed with the dust of the store formed a heavy layer over everything including the glass on the windows as well as showcases. His customers didn't mind, they usually came to him through word-of-mouth. They weren't here for the decor or the service. There weren't that many reliably unreliable gun dealers in this town. They knew he didn't ask too many questions about ID or what they did with the gun as long as they paid in full and paid in cash, with no bargaining. The store was in an unsavory part of town; the EL that ran overhead shook the building every 15 minutes during the day and every 40 minutes at night. The homeless and the drunk lined the dark street. It was not a place for the faint of heart. It was not uncommon for a mugging or two to happen every few days. The noise from the train may have bothered another person, but to Bob, it marked the time. It had even become comforting over the 13 years he had his shop. He had tried his hand at a nine-to-five job but figured after the first few months that he was not cut out for that. He had developed a dedicated clientele over the years. The space was cheap and he didn't have to sell many guns to pay his rent. The landlord didn't care too much about his business and didn't ask too many questions as long as he paid the rent on time. The day was slow, an odd customer came in and looked, but didn't buy. At 10 PM, Bob decided he had had enough. He usually at least stayed open till 11:30 or 12, but today he just couldn't concentrate. The memory of Ugrasena refused to leave his brain. What if he had a brain tumor? He had heard of people hearing and seeing things that weren't there and eventually being found to have large brain tumors. He decided to get things checked out. He had not been to the doctor in decades and usually didn't care much about his health. He decided to call his doctor's office first thing in the morning. Bob tossed and turned in bed, unable to sleep. He was usually a sound sleeper, but this night, he heard every train that went by and every street fight by the window. He remembered the soldiers chasing him down the narrow forest path, the pounding of his heart, the clanging of the sword that he carried on the side against his armor as he ran.

The staid decoration in the doctor's office was oddly calming. He waited, trying to figure out how he would explain to the doctor why he was here. They called his name and he went into the exam room. In a few minutes, a young doctor came in, looking more like a high school student than a doctor.

"Hi! I am Dr Patel," he introduced himself. Bob thought to himself, Great! Another foreign doctor. Hopefully, I can understand him. "So, Mr..." "Call me, Bob," he said, "Hi Bob, what can I do for you today?" asked Dr Patel. "I... had a headache yesterday," said Bob haltingly, "but I also can't remember what happened for some time." He saw the look of concern in Dr Patel's eyes. "Oh!" he said.

"I had this blank space where I don't remember what happened and then I had a headache afterward." As he continued, Bob hesitated. Should he tell him about the visions? He relived the incident as he spoke to the Doctor and as he spoke, he became more and more convinced that he was not imagining the whole thing. This was a waste of time. He got up, pushed past a startled Dr Patel and walked out of the office, ignoring the nurse yelling after him. "Sir... Sir ...!"

He wandered the streets the next day, seeing if he would have any other "staring" spells. He didn't, but he couldn't shake the image of Ugrasena from his brain either. He became certain as the day went on that this was not a tumor or a hallucination.

In spite of the cold, Bob walked the streets. The cold wind lashed his face but was refreshing. By late evening it had started to lightly snow. The snow slowly blanketed the street, making the sidewalk slick. He watched as cars slowly maneuvered the icy roads. Every now and then, an inexperienced driver would slam his brakes at a traffic light and crash into the car in front of him. *Pump the brakes, you idiot! thought Bob. Damn tourists! Chicago was now full of them.* He watched as pedestrians gingerly walked the icy sidewalks. He maintained a sure step and walked relatively briskly, dodging the crowds, one of the few skills he acquired over years of living in Chicago. He had been born in a town not far from the city, in one of the many smaller towns that surrounded the Chicago land area, called Valparaiso. A quiet and sleepy town of around 20,000, when he grew up.

Too quiet for him, he moved out to Chicago when his petty crimes started getting the attention of the local police. His father, the local high school teacher, was appalled. His midwestern mother even more so. They would ask repeatedly, both to him and of themselves, "Where did we go wrong?"

He had not spoken to them in years, well actually, more like in decades. In fact, he was not even sure they were alive.

They had their favorite son to care for them. This was the first time in years that he had even thought of them.

He made his way back to the shop and grabbed a sandwich on the way home. Watching the darkness envelope the city, he sat eating in front of the window. The hurrying crowds outside in the blowing snow made him feel all the more alone and insignificant. He had no one to hurry home for. Heck! Was a small room at the back of a store where he lived even a home?

He walked to the store. There was a man waiting by the door. He instinctively reached for his gun which he always carried and felt its a reassuring bulge. The man noticed the gesture and understood. "I need to get a gun," he said. "I am not selling today," said Bob.

"Why?" asked the man. "Because I don't feel like it," answered Bob coldly and stared him down till he walked away. He would be back, they always were. And even if he wasn't, Bob couldn't care less.

One question haunted him through the night: how can he get back? If he did, would he still be condemned to the same life, the life of a mercenary at the beck and call of every ruler, always on the run? What if... what if he could somehow make his life better? He had other visions, ones that didn't quite come to him with the vividity of Ugrasena and his life. The forest, the chasing soldiers. Somewhere at the back part of the brain he shared with Ugrasena, images of a king began to form; one that was formidable. With unprecedented power and wealth. This idea was barely even that. He couldn't tell whether this was even something that had formed in his brain or Ugrasena's. It was a like figment of a thought that had formed in the part of his brain that was becoming more and more melded with this memory of Ugrasena.

The pomp and splendor he witnessed in this vision and most importantly, the power that permeated him, were intoxicating.

This was something, the fact that he could even remember anything. Maybe he could take back some of his guns? Imagine ancient Indian battles fought with swords and elephants. Imagine people's faces when they see a gun. That gets people's attention pretty quickly. They would probably think he was some great warrior, maybe even a demigod with divine powers, and make him king, he laughed to himself. Why wait? He could, actually, make himself a king. *It would be like bringing a gun to a knife fight,* he thought and laughed. Bob knew he couldn't take a gun with him, but there had to be something. Something he could do to change the game dramatically. He reached for his laptop and opened a search page, his fingers poised on the keyboard as he thought hard. He typed 'greatest inventions of all time'. Wikipedia pulled up a list: the Internet, railroads, car. *No! No! That wouldn't do.* 'Inventions that changed the world', he typed and hit enter. Again, the Internet, cars, cotton, gin... *No, this was no good.* He cannot carry the Internet with him! He then typed 'inventions that changed warfare' and hit enter. He scanned through the results: the bow and arrow, the cannon, and then it leaped out at him, gunpowder. *Of course!* He can't carry a gun, but what if he could memorize the ingredients and then make gunpowder that would change everything? He would be invincible.

Chapter 14

Amit was getting better and better at controlling when and where he traveled. He now seemed to be able to travel without much effort, by merely closing his eyes for a few minutes and regulating his breathing. Mr Kailash had even seen him do it on a few occasions just staring into space.

The weather outside the ashram was getting cooler again, the mountains that surrounded the ashram would often have light snow on their highest peaks on some mornings. The tasks of the ashram kept Amit busy during the day. All the sadhus in residence took turns tending to the garden and doing the laundry as well as all the other tasks. The fertile Himalayan foothills soil was dark and rich and easily supplied the residents with fresh vegetables. In winter they stored the heartier vegetables. Amit was digging up potatoes in the ground with a pitchfork, carefully inserting it and turning up the soil and potatoes and bending to pick up the potatoes and put them in his basket. He dusted them off as he threw them in. He loved gardening the best. The fresh air, the smell of the moist soil, and the sun on his back invigorated him. He tried and tried to bring back some skills from his other lives but usually, the effect was fleeting. While he was able to travel freely between his lives, he found when he tried to wield a sword like the Rani for longer than a few minutes, his skills would rapidly fade. This was the next step—transferring and using knowledge and skills accrued over many lives and millennia. If he was able to do that, he stopped at the thought, it would be like he had a time machine that was able to transport skills from previous lives. Limited only by the skills he had truly acquired. Learning didn't have to be limited to one life but hundreds. This was exceedingly difficult and he struggled, growing more frustrated. It almost wanted to acquire his ability to travel had been far easier.

The time he demonstrated his skill with a sword to Mr Kailash was perhaps a fluke. His skills rapidly deteriorated with each passing minute of his being his present self. When he came back from Arya Bhatta, one of his more famous lives, a popular mathematician of ancient India, he found his mathematical skills were lost in less than an hour. The advanced algorithms he was looking at that, had made sense a few minutes ago and soon became unintelligible gibberish. He thought about this as he dug out the potatoes from the soil. He picked up his pitchfork and used his weight to drive the pitchfork into the ground by standing on the side. He then pulled up the earth, revealing 2 to 3 large potatoes. As he bent down to pick one up, he had an idea. Amit stared into space, standing still, waiting. He saw all his lives, in front of him like a beehive, with windows into his many existences. He then willed those lives into a blur, trying to imagine just each of their essences. Soon, in front of him, as though in a large imaginary chest of toys, lay the skills of each of his lives. Some, in fact, a lot, of his lives were 'ordinary', but a few of them had extraordinary achievements and skills.

Rani Mrignayani's sword lay there. Amit reached out and grabbed it. He willed himself to grab onto this imaginary sword and then bring it back to his reality. Amit looked around him and he was still standing in the field. The wind whispered gently in his ear. He looked down into his hands and there was no real sword. In his mind's eye, he still held it. He ran and grabbed a long stick on the ground and then brandished it. He waved it around in the air and it swished smoothly through the wind. He knew he had done it! He was elated. He ran, still brandishing the stick all the way down from the potato fields, past surprised sadhus who looked at him quizzically as he waved his stick in the air.

The guru looked up from the book she had been reading in the meditation hall.

"I did it!" yelled Amit loudly. The other sadhus in the room turned to him, annoyed, and shushed him. The guru smiled and said, "Well, we shall see." She turned to one of the sadhus sitting next to her, "Can you find Stan? Tell him we need him and his fencing swords." Stan was an Austrian sadhu who had been at the ashram for a few years. He was also an expert fencer, having gotten a few gold medals at the Olympics. Amit suddenly felt a twinge of anxiety. Had he promised too much? Did he really know what he was doing? From somewhere in the depths of his mind the answer was, yes!

As Stan walked in, he had two fencing swords with him. He was a 40-something athletic Scandinavian, still in great shape, especially in spite of the fact that he had not fenced competitively for more than 20 years. He looked at the Guru, perplexed. She whispered in his ear as he bent over her. Then a slow smile spread across his face. "This will be fun," he said as he stood up.

"Right, so we will be doing a fencing style called 'epee'," Stan addressed the group. "It is done traditionally with these—not swords, but 'epee'. This young man thinks he is a great swordsman. We shall see. I thought this might be the most appropriate game, given that it is closest to a battle scenario. In this, the whole body is a target, just like in a battle.

"All right, Amit, are you ready?" asked Stan. He threw the epee at Amit who caught it expertly and said, "Yes, I am!" without hesitation. "If I hit any part of your body, that counts as a point. In a battle that would mean you were stabbed with a sword in that part, so let's remember that."

The two faced off, circling each other warily. Amit moved around calmly, steadily, his weight well-balanced. Stan stared at him with an impenetrable gaze, not giving any clues of his intended moves. Suddenly, he lunged at Amit's right shoulder which was facing him. In battle, Amit, who was right-handed, would've been crippled if he was hit on his right shoulder. Amit lunged back and the blow just grazed his right shoulder. They circled again. Amit still did not make any aggressive moves. A steely look came into his eyes, one that the watching sadhus and the guru had not seen before. Stan again lunged, at Amit's left thigh this time, which Amit again dodged expertly. Stan was recovering from his lunge; his balance was forward with his sword thrust far out. Amit suddenly brought his sword with full force onto Stan's hand, knocking the sword right out of his hand. If this had been a battle and a real sword, his hand would've been sliced off cleanly. Stan jumped back, his hand stung as the sword clattered to the floor. Amit expertly rotated, following him as he reeled back, brought the sword to his neck, and stopped. Stunned silence followed, and then the surrounding sadhus clapped. Stan was beaming, in spite of his hand. "You were terrific," he said as he hugged Amit. "Believe me, I would know, I have three gold medals at the Olympics." The steely look in Amit's eyes slowly normalized; it was like he had come out of a trance. He looked at the Guru and she smiled. As the other sadhus dispersed, Amit sat down next to the Guru. She was thinking, and then she said, "So, do you think you can go and pick any skill from your previous lives like this?" "Yes," he said. "I know I can, I feel like they are laid out in a box. I can just pick one and hold it in my mind." "That is amazing! So, have you tried to return with more than one skill?" she asked. "Not yet," said Amit and smiled.

Chapter 15

B ob sat hunched over his computer as he had for the last several days. He had slept fitfully for several nights. Each night interrupted by dreams. Visions? He had not bothered opening the store and sat in the back bent over his laptop. A few customers banged and rattled the shutters, but he didn't bother with them. This was far more important. This was the chance of a lifetime. He smiled as he thought of a lifetime, this was the chance of two lifetimes. He read everything he could about gunpowder: the Chinese had invented it in the 19th century. Its use had slowly spread, its ingredients were relatively common and easy to manufacture. The Chinese had kept it a secret for a long time, but eventually, the secret leaked. It revolutionized warfare. Armies that faced off against Mongol hordes that had swept westward were terrified by the enormous blast that it was initially used for; the blast created panic. The armies facing it thought the Chinese had captured thunder and were using it as a weapon. Soon they had perfected cannons, using the explosive power to propel huge cannonballs powerful enough to destroy the greatest fortifications. Eventually, the Chinese figured out how to miniaturize the cannons. Hand cannons, they initially called them. Bob knew all about that, of course. The hand cannons were the first guns. This was incredible! This was the answer.

Now, of course, came the problem of how he would transport this knowledge back to Ugrasena's world. While he didn't know what century Ugrasena lived in, it was clearly before the invention of gunpowder. He tried as hard as possible to think of all the weapons the soldiers were armed with, but nothing came to his mind that could even be able to remotely rival cannons and gunpowder. His face lit up with joy, as he imagined himself taking on the local Raja and eventually establishing an empire. Right now though, he needed to get some fresh air. He also realized that he was ravenous. He turned on the light in the dark back room. It was completely dark outside. He looked at the dusty clock face on the wall, it was 10.30 PM. He put on a jacket and walked outside into the cool night air. It was refreshing after all these days inside. He walked to the diner on the corner. The bell on the door clanged as he entered, there was the usual late evening crowd of swing shift workers and drunks, in for a late meal. He walked to a corner booth, his usual spot, quiet and far from the hubbub in the front. The waitress looked at him from across the room and he nodded and she nodded back. She would bring him his usual order of eggs, bacon with some rye toast and heaps of butter on it, and, of course, coffee.

He closed his eyes, trying to figure out a way to be sure to carry this information back in time to Ugrasena. He could just remember the ingredients, but what if he forgot a crucial ingredient? The food arrived, the waitress laid out his usual meal. He had been eating the same thing for years, every night. He thanked her as she walked away and watched the steam rising from the coffee. He reached for the salt shaker. His hand knocked it down by mistake. The cap of the shaker must have been loose. It came off spreading salt over the table like a tiny blanket of snow. Bob picked up the shaker and screwed the cap on. He took his fork and began to twirl it mindlessly in the spilled salt, doodling spirals and circles in it.

"Of course!" It struck him. "That's it!" He would get a tattoo. He would tattoo all the ingredients of gunpowder, in addition to memorizing it. He recalled the first few minutes when he had returned to his body as Bob, he remembered the cuts and bruises suffered by Ugrasena. More and more he had recesses in his brain that he seemed to share with Ugrasena; he hoped that when he 'went back', he would continue to share that recess of his brain. His only hope would be if he could get back and quickly write down the ingredients. The important thing would be speed; he has to hold onto his thoughts for as long as he could when he returns, to give himself any chance. At least, there would be a chance that some remnant of this would carry through to Ugrasena. He didn't know if this would work, but this seemed to be as good an idea as any he had so far. He turned to his food with a renewed appetite. He now knew what he had to do the next morning. The bacon was crunchy, its flavor suddenly all the more vivid in his mouth.

Chapter 16

Bob stood outside the tattoo parlor hesitating for just a moment. He had imagined the expression on the tattoo artist's face when he mentioned what he wanted to be tattooed on his arm, but the man didn't blink an eye. In this age of gun nuts, another one was apparently not that uncommon. He had all the ingredients tattooed one by one, listed with the formula in the darkest ink they had. As the pain of the tattoo needle pierced his skin and his brain, he wondered how he would get to the banyan tree. The thinking would distract him from the pain. The banyan tree appeared to be critical to this somehow. Clearly, that was the way in and out. Maybe it was some sort of a portal. The tree itself appeared to be in India. All that he could recall of Ugrasena and his life suggested it. From what little he knew of the country, it was huge and filled with tons of people. How would he ever find the exact area of the country to find a tree? Where was it and did it still exist? Would the portal exist in absence of the tree? He doubted it, given what he remembered from climbing the tree and specifically going to the third branch. This was obviously centuries earlier. The stinging pain of the needle made him wince. He would have to think of everything he could recall on Ugrasena, or anything at all that might offer a clue, a clue as to where this banyan tree might be. He thrust the $150 in cash into the tattoo artist's hand, his arm still smarting from the pain of the needle. Why would people do this for fun? *Idiots,* he thought.

I need a computer, a piece of paper and a pen, he thought. He went back to the store. It was late afternoon. Two somewhat unsavory men were hanging out by the front but that was most of his clientele. He ushered the two guys in and they followed him into the store. It was the usual. They wanted to see a few semi-automatic guns. They clearly weren't hunters or even gun enthusiasts, but he didn't care. He charged a premium and they paid. He didn't ask any questions and they didn't haggle about the price. That was the deal he had with his customers. He folded the crumpled bills they thrust into his hands and shut the door behind them, making sure they walked away, and pulled down the shutters. Turning off the open sign, he sat in his backroom in darkness and tried to think. He needed to reimagine and write down everything he could remember about Ugrasena, everything about where he lived and what he did. He remembered the soldiers chasing him. His heart began to beat faster at the very thought. He could hear the hooves pounding, the sound of his heart as it beat out of his chest. The banyan tree. Where was this? He tried, but all he could remember was that he was Ugrasena, a mercenary who was being chased by the king's soldiers.

His head throbbed as he concentrated hard; it was like he kept banging his head on the wall, trying to remember beyond the part where the soldiers chased him into the clearing where the banyan tree stood. He needed to think backward, rewind Ugrasena's life as they did in the movies. He wished it was that easy. He lay down on his couch, his mind exhausted by the effort of trying to remember. He fell into a fitful sleep.

He woke up with a start a few hours later. Yes, of course, he was from Kalinga. He had been born there; it all came back. He remembered falling into a life of petty crime. He remembered his father was a cobbler, he remembered his look of disappointment when Ugrasena was brought home by the local soldiers in chains after having committed his first crime. His mother had always tried to make excuses for him, but when he stole from the neighbor's house to settle a gambling debt, even she had had enough and he was thrown out of the house. He had left Kalinga and gone to the neighboring Koshala kingdom and signed up in the army as an infantryman. The infantrymen were the cannon fodder of battles. They lived their lives not knowing that every day could well be their last. Infantrymen were usually the rough and ready sort of people whom society had rejected for one reason or another. He fit right in, the few morals his pious father had instilled in him were soon rubbed out of him by the army and the company he kept. Any qualms he had fell by the wayside.

He knew he had to get out of this life or he would be the next corpse on the battlefield. When the Koshala king declared war on Kalinga, the opportunity fell into his lap. The army Commander lined up the battalion of infantrymen and explained the battle plan. It was the usual do-it-for-God-and-country nonsense. The more he heard the speech, the less he believed it. He stood to attention as required but was startled when his battalion commander called his name. It appeared that some of them were being chosen for another task.

He took 50 of them aside and had another job for them. He was chosen for his skills with his sword. There was to be a surprise attack—Ugrasena and 49 other men would sneak through a secret tunnel in the forest that led to the inside of the walls of the Kalinga fort. The attack was to happen at two in the morning. Ugrasena and the rest were instructed to get some rest as the sun slowly set in the distance. Ugrasena went to his tent that he shared with two other men. The two men, Balasena and Pratihara, were local Koshala lads who knew each other from childhood. They were good sort but too nice to be friends with Ugrasena. They had reached the tent before him and were discussing the plans for the secret raid. The two of them believed the nonsense that was being peddled to them about the love of king and country. They were eager to make their mark on the world, their eyes shining with the excitement of the coming assault. This annoyed Ugrasena. This was not about the love of country, this was about two greedy kings fighting a turf battle. He knew all too well that the king and the army chief did not care whether he lived or died and barely knew him by face, leave alone by name. His comrades decided to turn in early to get some rest. As they slowly dozed off Ugrasena lay on his bed. He knew this was an opportunity that he could not lose. For once in his life, he'd been given something, an opportunity, a gift. A gift of information, information that was vital to the rival army who would pay a handsome price for this. As he heard the heavy breathing of the other two, Ugrasena slowly crept out of the tent. A hush had fallen on the camp and the campfires were dying out. All he could hear were a few drunken soldiers laughing in the distance. He walked quietly to the stables. He guessed by the clear night sky that it was about 11 or so; it would take an hour of hard riding to reach Koshala.

He had to hurry. He untied the fastest appearing horse and led it out of the camp through the back. As soon as he was a few hundred feet away from the camp, he got on the horse and rode it hard, through the forest path between Koshala and Kalinga. The dense darkness of the forest meant he could barely see, but he knew this area well, almost like the back of his hand. He had been on this path many times. He prayed he didn't run into a wild animal. As he approached the boundaries of the Kalinga kingdom, he knew he would be greeted by guards at the gate, which would surely be closed. This is where he hoped his history would come in handy. The gates were closed. The guards were perched high up on the watchtowers above the gate, its imposing wooden frame towering above him. There were a few people camped outside the gate, cooking on small fires as they sat waiting for the dawn when the gate would open again. But he couldn't wait. He looked up at the night sky, it must be close to 12 or even later. Soon, the Koshala army would start towards the tunnel.

He shouted to the guards, "Open the gate." They looked down, annoyed at the noise. "What do you want? You have to wait until morning, like everyone else. Don't you know the gate closes at sunset and opens at sunrise?" "I have urgent news for the commander in chief or the king," said Ugrasena. "I need to see them right away."

"Right!" said the soldier, "And I want a hundred gold Mohurs. We don't always get what we want! Go away!"

Ugrasena shouted again with rising desperation, "If I don't see the chief right away, many men will die! My father is Balarama Sena. I'm a resident of Kalinga, I have valuable information." The soldiers now were undecided. It sounded serious and real, and *anyway, they thought, it was one soldier. What harm could he do alone?* Ugrasena waited impatiently as he could see them arguing back and forth. They opened a small side door in the main gate and told Ugrasena to come in. He heaved a sigh of relief. As he walked through the gate, he thought he was about to be very rich. He smiled to himself. The soldiers immediately grabbed his sword away from him and marched him to the commander's room. Ugrasena knew the hardest part was still ahead, convincing the commander to hear out his plan. As he walked into the commander's hut, he tried to quickly come up with something he could say that would get his attention. Time was running out; the soldiers would set off for the tunnel in less than an hour.

The guards knocked nervously on the door with no answer. Finally, after several hard knocks, an extremely grumpy man opened the door, he wasn't happy. Ugrasena blurred out, "If you give me 150 gold Mohurs, I can win this war for you!"

The commander, a wizened old man with an enormous mustache, laughed a hearty belly laugh! 150 gold Mohurs! "Who is this idiot?" he said as he turned angrily to his guards. "Why are you wasting my time? I have to get some rest. I have a battle to prepare for."

"You must listen to me!" said Ugrasena with a growing sense of desperation. He couldn't throw away the one chance he had, it was now or never. "Please listen to me," pleaded

Ugrasena. "Hang me if I'm wrong. But if I'm right, well, reward me 150 gold Mohurs!"

The commander was a battle-hardened man and knew battles turned on a dime. Maybe this soldier really had the right information. All he had to do was hang him if he was lying, to make him an example to other idiots who would bother to wake him up, promising bogus information. He looked at the two nervous guards standing next to Ugrasena. He would hang them for good measure too.

"All right," he said, "150 gold Mohurs. What do you have?" Ugrasena quickly blurted out his information all about the tunnel. He emphasized that time was running out. The commander's expression suddenly changed and he became a battle veteran immediately. He barked orders as he walked, putting on his dark leather and metal armor. "Where did you say the tunnel opened?" he turned to Ugrasena. "At the base of the peepal tree, behind the northern well," Ugrasena said quickly. The commander knew what he had to do; he would counterattack. He ordered one battalion of soldiers to hide all around the well, armed to the teeth. He dispatched his best cavalry battalions to ride hard to attack the camp of the Koshala army. While they sat waiting for the secret attack to take place, he would attack them from behind. They wouldn't know what hit them. Ugrasena felt relieved. He knew his job was done; all he could do now was wait.

The commander turned to him. "You are my guest till this is done," he said with a grim smile. He ordered the soldiers to lock him up in the dungeon until he sent for him.

After all the excitement of the last few hours, Ugrasena found himself staring at the blackness of the dungeon. He paced the 5 x 8 structure as best as he could in the darkness of the dungeon. He could hear the rats scurry away as he walked towards them. Ugrasena tried as hard as he could to hear a single sound from the surface. The hours ground by glacially, the sun must've come up for ages. It was still dark in the dungeon. As his eyes adjusted to the light in the dungeon, it became a hazy gray from a pitch black. He was hungry and exhausted but could not bring himself to sit for more than a few minutes. At last, he heard footsteps and he jumped up. It was the same two guards; they had a smile on their face. Was it a smile at his imminent death or one of their own victory? He heard the clang of the jail door as it opened with a creak, the sound ringing out against the stone walls. A few prisoners moaned pitifully at the sound. Who knew how long they had been there? The soldiers looked at him.

"What happened?" he asked. "It was a massacre, we chopped them down as they came up, one after the other, through that tunnel. The rest of the Koshala army was decimated by a surprise attack. They surrendered, Koshala is ours!" His gamble had paid off, Ugrasena smiled a broad smile as he thought of the gold Mohurs, all 150 of them.

The guards led him to the commander's hut. He was sitting outside in the shade of a tree looking exhausted. His armor was stained with blood, he had a gash running down his right arm that was covered with clotted blood. When he saw Ugrasena, he beckoned one of the guards sitting next to him. The guard went into his hut and came back with a small bag. The commander threw it at Ugrasena. "Here you go." His face had a look of disgust. Ugrasena was surprised as he was expecting gratitude. He opened the bag and peered in it. It was all there, the glint of gold flashed up at him. The commander said, "There's only one way you could've come by that information, take this money and get out of my kingdom. I don't want to see your face ever again! I hate traitors but I also love the smell of victory." He turned to the guards, "Throw him out of the fort!" The guards led Ugrasena out of the fort and one of them, out of pity, gave him his horse back. Ugrasena was thrilled, this had been too easy. He didn't care what the commander thought of him. He hadn't cared for all the curses. If even his mother's curses hurled at him about eternal damnation and infamy hadn't hurt him, what was another man's ire? He knew if these curses worked, he would have been long dead.

He rode through the busy central thoroughfare in the town. Festive buntings were being hung, loud raucous celebrations could be heard in the houses and bars. Some people danced in joy in the streets. Little did people realize that he was responsible for this victory. He wanted to tell them but he knew they wouldn't believe him. Probably would think he was drunk. As he rode out of the kingdom, he realized he was famished; he hadn't eaten anything for almost an entire day. The adrenaline of the last few hours had kept him going. He knew he needed to get out of the kingdom first. Where would he go? Clearly, he couldn't go back to Koshala. The world was his oyster; he could go wherever he chose, now that he had money. He had never in his life been in this situation, with lots of money and nothing to do. He remembered the path that led to a roadside shack. Where an old woman sold food, usually whatever simple fare she had made that day. He had been there in the past. He slowed his horse as he came upon the stall.

The old woman who ran it sat by a fire over which there was a large metal dish. There was no one else at the stall,

Ugrasena was glad. She looked like she hadn't aged at all; she had looked a hundred then and looked about the same now. How long had it been since he had seen her? 5 years, maybe more?

He asked for some water for his horse. As the horse drank, Ugrasena also asked the woman for a plate of idlis. As he sat on a little wooden stool waiting for his food, his hand was rubbing the bag of money at his side. Should he travel out of the country to see the world? He would first have to get out of this area, it was too easy to be spotted by the jealous soldiers, or worse, stragglers from the vanquished Koshala army. The first thing for a road trip was a full stomach. It had been a long time since he had eaten. He went through a mound of idlis, their warmth comforting him. He made the woman put a generous amount of ghee on top. Soldiers were usually given dry plain rations and the ghee tasted luxurious in his mouth. A sign of things to come, he smiled to himself.

Ugrasena asked for some oats for his horse. He would need it for the journey. He also needed water; the old lady gave him some. He pressed a silver coin into her hand, far more than needed. "When someone asks whether you saw a man go this way, what do you say?" She smiled a toothless smile at him and shook her head no.

She had seen desperados before and understood. He took his bag of oats and his water bag and slung them over his horse. He turned one last time to look at the receding fort of Kalinga in the distance. Childhood memories rushed through his head. The beatings and the poverty of his childhood were what he remembered most. He hated the place. *It was time to move on,* he thought as he kicked his horse into a gallop. He rode hard and fast for the first 8 to 10 miles. Unfortunately, he had to go by the Koshala kingdom before the path turned away and he knew he would be in trouble if any of the defeated Koshala soldiers ran into him. He approached the outskirts of the kingdom of Koshala. Maybe he could skirt its borders and get lucky. The road became narrower and soon nothing more than a path in the woods. The sun was setting in the distance and his horse would need some rest soon, he slowed to a canter through the dry jungle brush. He was now in Koshala territory.

He heard some voices in the distance. He slowed his horse and rode into a small clearing in the woods. They were four of five soldiers gathered around a fire; they were cooking some food in a small pot. One of them leaned over the pot and stirred. As his horse stepped into the clearing, the men jumped up, swords drawn. The man who had been stirring the pot looked startled and reached for his sword. As he saw Ugrasena, the look on his face turned to shock. It was Pratihara, the young soldier who had shared a tent with Ugrasena in the camp. Ugrasena knew there was no room for error. He had to convince them he had been there all along. He did not see Balasena, Pratihara's friend, but he could be anywhere. Pratihara himself appeared to be hurt. He had his left arm in a bloody sling. "Ugrasena!" he said. *Good, maybe they didn't suspect anything,* thought Ugrasena. He got off his horse and approached the fire. He tried to strike what he hoped was a casual air. "That was some battle," he said. "Where is Balasena?"

Pratihara looked at him. His facial expression mingled with sadness, and was that suspicion? Ugrasena couldn't see his face as clearly as he would've liked. Pratihara said slowly, "He died."

Good riddance, thought Ugrasena. He had never liked that little know-it-all. With all this talk of kingdom and country and other patriotic nonsense. Pratihara looked at him keenly, his eyes slit as he spoke.

"Where were you? You were supposed to come with us to the tunnel Ugrasena. We woke up and you weren't there."

"What are you talking about? I went ahead," said Ugrasena.

"Ahead where?" said Pratihara. "They knew we were coming. It appeared as if somebody had warned them. We were massacred! Everyone thinks there was a traitor, someone who warned them of our arrival. They even knew where we had camped exactly, they attacked by surprise. So many died that we were lucky to get away." As he continued speaking, he slowed down. His voice became steelier by the minute. He then spat out, "No one, not one of us, escaped unhurt." As Pratihara talked, Ugrasena noticed from the corner of his eye that a few of the other soldiers slowly started walking behind him. Pratihara continued, "What's in that bag at your waist?" he asked. These men may have been soldiers but Ugrasena was a rogue. He had cheated many people in his life and sometimes things didn't go well. He always had to watch his back. He did not need to hear anymore. He turned and in one quick motion, got onto his horse and rode as hard as he could. He heard shouting but did not look back, he knew what was going to happen. He heard the whizzing before he saw the arrows, the soldiers continued to shoot them. One of the arrows whizzed by his ear as the path turned. He knew he would have a little respite as he was out of sight. On the other hand, he knew it would be a matter of minutes before they got on to the horses and rode after him. He had to get as much distance between them and him as possible. Suddenly his horse started slowing down, she was flagging that she couldn't be that tired already. He tried to goad her on but she didn't respond. He looked behind and saw that she had three arrows in her flank. The horse buckled under him and he was thrown to the ground. He rolled off smoothly and ran as quickly as he could without stopping. He reached a fork in the path and continued running as fast as he could. He ran for what felt like an hour. He was exhausted and he would need to stop soon. He panted past a stone arch into a clearing where a large banyan tree stood.

Bob woke up with a start! The arch, Kalinga! Maybe that would help him identify the banyan tree. He ran to a computer. How long has he been asleep? He looked at the clock on the wall. It read 11, daylight streamed in through the dusty windows. Kalinga? Where was this? He fired up his computer, impatiently watching the windows icon come on, and of course, he needed an update. He watched increasingly frustrated as the little progress bar went from 0 to 100% exceedingly slowly. He opened Google as soon as he could and typed Kalinga into it. Wikipedia had several articles about the Kalinga Empire, apparently a large powerful empire until Ashoka came by. The more he read, the more he was intrigued and he opened Google Maps to look up Kalinga. Its capital, Toshali, was an extremely well laid-out, prosperous town. There it was! The old fort! He recognized the ramparts as he imagined Ugrasena looking up at them. If he had ridden out of the capital on the main road leading out, he would have ridden about 30 to 40 miles out. He read maps from the Archaeological Society of India. He tried to study their projections of where the capital would be in modern India. He pored over the location of the capital and its structures and roads. He tried to imagine himself on the map. How he would've ridden out of the capital, trying to impose his memory of the surroundings from his imagination of them on the map. He switched to satellite mode; the country had obviously changed, the forest had given way to an urban jungle. It took immense concentration to imagine forests instead of buildings. As he opened the satellite mode, he looked in the vicinity of the kingdom of yore and saw the massive structures of the Konark temple, the dot-like people that killed around the grounds of the temple, frozen forever in mid-activity. Their numbers suggested it was a popular tourist attraction. Black Pagoda, it had been called by the British. He could see why it must be an impressive structure from the ground. As he moved the cursor around randomly, he saw what could only be a banyan tree! It appeared to be in the courtyard of the sun temple of Konark, a structure that must have come up later. But it was unmistakable, it was the same banyan tree from memory. He knew what he had to do. He opened up a travel website and booked a ticket for India.

Chapter 17

As the plane touched down in Delhi, Bob was exhausted. He wasn't into flying and most of his vacations, if you could call them that, consisted of road trips back-and-forth from his mother's house in St. Louis. He had never even thought of India, leave alone contemplate visiting. All he knew of the country was that it existed and that it was hot and crowded. He had never been much of a history buff. Left that for the nerds in the class. As he got off the plane, he wondered for a second if he was just crazy. If you had told him a week or two ago that he would be in India, looking for an ancient banyan, tree to travel to his past life, he would've laughed in your face and probably called the cops. He made a connecting flight to Bhuvneshwar and from there hired a taxi to take to Konark. He knew the taxi driver was ripping him off but he had no urge to haggle with him. The journey had worn him down, he otherwise was not a man who enjoyed getting ripped off. Also, he couldn't care less about a few rupees now that he was so close to his dream. The humid air was stifling. He couldn't have chosen a worse time for his first trip to India. The weather in May in Odisha before the monsoon was thick and the city pollution seemed to leave a sticky layer on him. *The humidity is probably close to 100%,* he thought, wiping the sweat off his forehead. He marveled at the people, fully covered, walking down the crowded streets of the city. The heat didn't seem to bother them. Even more surprising he saw stalls where sweaty men sat stirring hot cauldrons of tea. Customers thronged the stalls, buying and drinking the hot tea that was dispensed in tiny clay pots.

The AC in the car struggled to keep up. As their cars snailed through the crowded streets of Bhubaneswar, the driver repeatedly leaned heavily on his horn. In fact, everyone seemed to be doing the same. The streets were crowded with a myriad of cars, scooters, motorcycles, and rickshaws, all seemingly communicating with each other with horns, bells, and curses. As the car left the city, the roads opened up. The heat seemed to improve marginally as the pollution of the city lifted and the air became clearer. The driver didn't seem to realize he was driving an actual car rather than a plane or playing a video. He hurtled down the brand-new expressway and screeched to a halt at the toll gate. Every time a jet-lagged Bob dozed off to sleep, he was jerked violently awake.

He had left Bhubaneswar in the evening and by the time they reached Konark, it was late in the night. He was exhausted. He needed some rest. The banyan tree would have to wait till the morning; anyway, he wouldn't be able to find his way in the dark and it was probably closed. *It had only been a few millennia since he had been here,* he thought wryly.

The car pulled up to a modest hotel. *Kamala Nivas,* its dusty sign read. The lobby was clean and the floor was shining. There was a man with a dirty mop and a bucket swabbing the floor. He looked up with minimal interest at the new arrival. Foreign tourists were quite common in this part of the country. The smell of phenol permeated the air. Mildly unpleasant.

The AC in the hotel lobby was welcoming. It was a hotel recommended by his cab driver and was certainly adequate. All he had wanted was functioning air conditioning. The bellboy smiled effusively at him and took his bags after he had checked in. 2000 rupees for a room, his tired brain tried to do the math in dollars, certainly not more than $30 a night. *Not bad,* he thought. He had stayed in places a lot worse than this and paid a lot more. The bellboy led him to his room. The elevator wasn't working, so he was taken up a stairway with peeling paint on the walls. The room was surprisingly spacious and smelt of cheap soap and cleaning solution. The bellboy smiled a servile smile. Bob reached into his pocket and shoved a few single dollar bills into the bellboy's hand. He was happy and thanked him profusely as he backed out of the door. Bob was exhausted. He quickly showered, the weak shower dripped more than sprayed and he was barely able to get the soap off. He didn't bother changing and collapsed onto the bed in his towel. He did not have the energy to find food. He had a deep dreamless sleep, for the first time in several days. When he finally woke up, it was already nine and the sunlight streamed through the curtain, hitting him in the eye. He was a little irritated with himself for having not gotten up at the crack of dawn as he had hoped. He quickly got dressed. He needed to get to the temple. He walked to the reception. A well-dressed Indian woman in a sari greeted him with a big smile. "Hello sir, how can I help you?" she asked in perfect English, surprising him. "I need to go to the Konark temple." "Of course," she said, "our number one tourist attraction. I can find you a reliable cab." She picked up the phone and spoke in Oriya rapidly. As she hung up, she turned to him and said, "Your cab will be out in a few minutes, sir."

As he made his way out to the portico, the heat was already stifling. He felt like he was walking into a wall of warm mist. The cab didn't have air-conditioning and he rolled down the window, his face awash with the humid breeze and a hundred smells that he didn't recognize. The cab weaved in and out of the traffic. He was continually amazed at the controlled chaos around him and even more so by the drivers' undoubted skill in maneuvering the chaos. They eventually pulled up to the temple.

It was a fantastical structure and loomed large over the skyline, a magnificent ruin. The gate in front of the temple teemed with guides, touts, and tourists. They had set up makeshift stalls and tables in the shade of the trees in the large area in front of the temple. Large tour buses huffing and honking pulled up. Auto rickshaws pulled up with people literally spilling out of them. The guides recognized a foreigner immediately and besieged him with offers of tours and special deals. He shook them off by walking briskly and purposefully. The temple had a perimeter. This went around the entire circumference of the temple. The walkway was lined with red dirt and irregularly placed stones. He had little interest in the temple itself; he needed to find the tree. As he walked briskly around the perimeter, he tried to imagine the area as it must've been 2500 years ago. The trees that would've dominated the area, were now few and far between. He had walked around to the back of the massive structure. Its massive central pagoda had collapsed at the top. It was surrounded by several smaller pagodas in various states of ruin and collapse. As he turned the corner, he came upon it. It was unmistakable, the huge canopy of the banyan tree burst into view. It was ancient, its main trunk had several secondary trunks, each of them massive in their own right. The entire tree covered no less than a few hundred feet; people were sprawled on blankets, picnicking in its shade. Bob broke into a run, the excitement overwhelmed him. All he had to do was climb into its branches. He saw the very branch from where he had fallen. As he approached the trunk, he noticed several hundred threads in bright yellow and red that hung from the tree, adding a splash of color to it. He didn't pay any attention to the surrounding people; he would be gone to his old life in a few minutes. His heart pounded with anticipation. The onlookers were surprised as he ran past them, a white man in a sea of brown bodies with streams of sweat dripping down his face. He tried to get a head start by jumping onto one of the lower branches. No sooner had he put his foot on the base and began to pull himself up than an uproar broke out amongst the crowd. Several of the men closest to him grabbed and yelled angrily at him. The women in colorful saris stood up, their faces contorted with anger. People grabbed his feet and pulled him off the tree. There was much shoving and pushing as he was roughed up by the crowd. They yelled at him in the local language. Even if he didn't understand the language, he could gather that they were not pleased. Finally, one of them, a middle-aged man with a paunch and large mustache, pushed his way through the crowd and addressed him in English.

"Are you crazy? You can't climb this tree. Don't you know it's a holy banyan tree? How dare you to climb it? And that too, with shoes no less," he said. The man grabbed his arm and led him away from the angry mob. He went on to explain that he committed sacrilege by stepping onto the tree. The red threads he had seen, tied to the tree, had been tied by women for good luck. The tree was considered to be holy and therefore forbidden to climb. Bob was seething; he couldn't believe his terrible luck. Here he was, against all odds, standing in front of 'the tree' that would take him back to a bright rich past and he was being denied by some ridiculous local customs. As he turned away, shook up, he was determined to come back. He would come back tonight, surely it would be abandoned then. He would climb it and reach his destiny. Bob rode a taxi back to his hotel. He was hot and angry and needed to get some rest. The jet lag and the heat had made him exhausted. He went up to his room and ordered some food. He flipped on the TV and clicked through channels and channels of shows in languages he didn't understand. His mind was set on finding a way to go back to the tree. He decided he would go at around 1 AM. Surely it would be abandoned.

Kautilya walked purposefully into the clearing in the jungle. There was the large banyan tree, its branch spreading all across the clearing, its enormous proportions looming even larger in the fading light. As Kautilya approached the tree, he looked around. He knew what or who he was looking for this time. The old woman came around the tree. Sabari was smiling, he recalled the first time he had met her and how different his reaction had been. She smiled at him, somewhat weakly, and the dog stood by her side. They knew what they had to do. It was the only way. They also knew that they had to do it fast. Kautilya went into the forest and picked up dry branches. He worked fast; he made several large piles, the largest at the base of the tree.

"Do you think we have enough branches?" he asked Sabari, she looked up from the pile she was arranging.

"I'm not sure. We can't afford to make a mistake, let's get some more branches," she said. He walked quickly into the woods to gather as many branches as he could carry. The two worked silently, purposefully. The massive pile of dry twigs and branches now almost touched the first branch of the tree. It was hard work and Kautilya was drenched in sweat.

"I think we are ready," said Sabari. She struck a flintstone to create a spark and soon had the fire going at the base of the tree. Kautilya took a few flaming branches and lit several other fires. They watched as the blaze slowly picked up. Soon, they could no longer stay anywhere near the tree.

Kautilya helped Sabari move back into the forest to a safe distance. They watched as the flames first engulfed the lower branches and then the upper branches. They had been fortunate that it was the dry season and there had been no rain for months. The tree eventually was a blazing beacon in the forest. The heat from the huge blaze could be felt for hundreds of feet around. Sabari looked at Kautilya with a sad look in her eyes. "It is done," she said.

Bob woke up to the chirping of his phone alarm. 1 AM it was time. He got dressed quickly, the night had cooled the city. It was actually pleasant for the first time since he had come to India. A gentle breeze was blowing through the window that he had left open last night. He had not bothered to change, knowing he would need to get moving quickly. He ran down to the hotel lobby, it was empty. He turned to the reception where a woman sat dozing on a chair. He dinged the small bell on the counter. The woman woke up with a start. To her credit, she smiled through her sleep. He asked for a cab to the temple, gruffly. The receptionist looked at him puzzled. "Sir, it's closed now and won't open till around 8 AM," she said. This was a different woman but just as polite.

"No, that's all right. I just need to take some pictures. You see, I love photography at night and the moonlight is perfect tonight," said Bob. "I thought it would make for some incredible pictures. Will there be anyone there now?" he asked, trying to sound casual. "You see, I just want a clear picture with nothing but the temple."

"Of course, I would be happy to help, sir. There will be absolutely no one there now, sir." she smiled, probably thinking, *these crazy tourists*. She made a quick phone call for a cab. The woman had to try several agencies before she could get him one. He waited another 20 minutes before it finally showed up. The driver looked bleary-eyed.

"You want to go to the temple now, sir?" he asked incredulously. Bob explained his photography fascination to him again, trying hard to keep his cool. He had enough of this country and he needed to get to his destiny. He was getting impatient.

In the cab, Bob thought to himself, *this was going to work, at last!* He rolled down the window and felt the cool breeze refreshing his face. Ugrasena would be a powerful king with nothing and nobody to stop him. The roads were much quieter and emptier; the driver only had to dodge some stray dogs on the road. They reached the temple in no time. Even as he got off the taxi from the main gate, he could see that something was wrong. The firetrucks in the front were not a good sign. He quickly paid the cab driver and ran up to the open gate. There was a hubbub of activity and Bob slipped in through the chaos, the policeman and firefighters too busy to care. *What had happened?* He ran to the back of the temple as fast as he could, as he approached the turn for the tree. He knew he was too late. All that was left of the tree was a massive smoldering carcass. The debris of the blaze was strewn all around the trunk. Ash billowed in the air. The once-massive tree was blackened and charred, most of its branches had collapsed, the heat was still immense and hit his face. He sank to his knees, tears rolling down his face. It was gone, all gone!

He grabbed a passing firefighter by the hand. "What happened?" he asked the man.

The firefighter irritably said, "We don't know, it apparently suddenly burst into flames and in a matter of minutes, the entire tree was engulfed. Luckily, no one was hurt and more importantly, the temple itself is unharmed." The fireman backed away from Bob, surprised to see a white man in tears for an old banyan tree.

Chapter 18

Amit and Mr Kailash looked at each other, exhausted. It was done. Had they done the right thing? There had been no other way. As Amit got up, he noticed they were surrounded by other sadhus meditating. The Guru sat meditating in the center, she sensed him and opened her eyes. She looked at Amit and Mr Kailash and smiled. She knew they had done what she had told them to do. The other sadhus began to rouse from their meditations and filed out slowly from the meditation hall.

Amit was ravenous and smelt the food before he saw it, they had been prepared. He began to eat the food that was waiting for him, warm idlis and sambar never felt as good as they did then. Mr Kailash said to him, "For a change, Amit, I am as hungry as you are this time," as he too dug into the food. The guru sat and watched them, smiling gently. As they finished and washed their hands, Amit came and sat by the Guru.

"Do you have questions, Amit?" she asked. "Where do I begin, did we do the right thing by burning the tree? Are there more such portals?" he asked "Amit, you did what you had to do, clearly there was no other way. Bob would've been a disaster for the people and the world if he managed to carry out his plan. You managed to preserve *this* future. Are there other portals? I'm not sure, what I do know is that we must remain vigilant. This has happened in the past and will surely happen again. As long as we have guardians like you and Kailash, we will be able to prevent other evildoers from stumbling onto them and destroying the life continuum. You asked me what the purpose of your powers was, do you understand now? Sometimes that will involve making difficult decisions. In the months, years and centuries I have known you..." she smiled at the thought. Centuries, yes, she had known him in various forms forever. "I know that you have and will make the right decisions in the past, present, and the future. For you, Amit, are the Guardian of Time," the Guru finished. Amit smiled. He liked the sound of that.

Epilogue

The girl was backing slowly away from the man. He had a small dagger in his hand, the light from the moon gleamed off the steel blade. She was about 7 years old or so, certainly not any more than that. She wasn't sure why she was being chased but she didn't want to wait to find out. The expression on the man's face was enough explanation. She had noticed him following her from school. He was ordinary appearing, but something about his face, ordinary as it was, gave away his intent. Maybe it was because of her generally suspicious nature. She hadn't always been this way, but since her parents died two years ago, she had been unusually unlucky. The time at the fairground was still fresh in her mind. After her parent's death, she had begun living with her aunt and uncle. This was her mother's sister and her family. Every time she looked at her aunt, little bits of her mother seemed to peer back, the slant of the head, the laugh, the way she walked. They were wonderful people, but she suspected that they thought she was strange, forever collecting dead insects of various kinds that she carried with her in little jars and bags, taking great care not to damage them. She recalled the look of slight disgust and worry when they saw how excited she was to see the dead butterfly on the ground and was amazed that she picked it up very carefully without any fear. The butterfly was perhaps easier to understand, less easy to comprehend was her love of collecting dead flies. They were puzzled to see that she was completely unafraid.

The man was as puzzled to see her open her backpack carefully. She was clearly backed into a corner in the alley. He had made sure he was forced into a relatively abandoned one in the city. Surely, she couldn't have a weapon in that bag, she was 7! He slowed down nevertheless, not taking any chances. His instructions were to bring her to them alive. He didn't need the girl doing anything stupid. The job was a simple one: pick her up without any drama and bring her to them. The girl continued unzipping the backpack, unperturbed. She pulled out a small can, it was a can of Pringles. The man looked surprised. *Was she going to eat a snack... now?* He hesitated as she opened the can of Pringles and gently removed something. He couldn't see what it was, it was small and colorful. No more than a few centimeters in size. *Nothing to worry about*, he thought, as he again began to walk towards her. The girl looked at him as he approached and suddenly stared into space. The bag in her hand dropped along with the can of Pringles. It clattered to the ground, the metal of the can clanging on the street floor, the sound ringing against the narrow walls of the alley. She crumpled lifelessly to the ground. A butterfly with bright yellow wings fluttered away. Even while taking in the shock, the man was surprised to see the butterfly in this grimy alley. Perhaps it was startled from the corner by the bag. *Oh my god! Did she have a seizure?* he thought as he ran to her. He shook her lifeless body. Nothing! He then took her pulse on her wrist and then as he had seen in so many TV shows on what he assumed was her carotid. Nothing! Panic ran through the man's mind; he had done nothing. They had explicitly said *alive*.

He was now afraid; he turned and ran, making sure as he left the alley that no one saw him, glancing furtively on both sides before he stepped out and melted into the darkness.

The girl's body lay on the ground, still lifeless. The butterfly fluttered about occasionally, finally landing on the backpack.

A man entered the alley, a different man. He was wearing a pair of jeans and a simple t-shirt. He was around 40 years or so. He had a look of concern in his eyes as he walked surely to the girl's body. He knelt by it. He had a kind look on his face. He said aloud, "It's okay. You can trust me. I can help you."

He looked around and his eyes rested on the butterfly that was sitting on the backpack. He smiled and said, "It is safe now!" seemingly to the butterfly. He said it again and again. The butterfly slowly ceased, fluttering its wings. It landed on the backpack and became completely still and lifeless. The girl stirred, suddenly, gasping for breath. Soon she settled down and sat up slowly. She looked at him with her large brown eyes filled with a little fear but mostly surprise.

"Shh. Don't worry. I am a friend," he said. "My name is Amit."

About the Author

Vinay Chakravarthy has been an avid history buff and a lover of Amar Chitra Katha as a child. He loves fantasy and Indian mythology, as well as a rollicking rebirth saga. He has brought these varied interests to bear on his latest book.

He draws on these childhood inspirations and his general love of travel to bring a tale that begins like a *Chandamama* story and then goes on to explore themes of life and death, birth and rebirth.

In his real life, he can be found tending to the living as a Physician and in the company of his family and cats.

www.ingramcontent.com/pod-product-compliance
Lightning Source LLC
LaVergne TN
LVHW051543170726
843492LV00006B/1923